Beauty
Sleep

Books by Hildegarde Dolson

Mysteries:

Beauty Sleep
Please Omit Funeral
A Dying Fall
To Spite Her Face

Other Books:

Heat Lightning
Open the Door
We Shook the Family Tree
Guess Whose Hair I'm Wearing
The Great Oildorado
Sorry to Be so Cheerful
The Form Divine
How About a Man?
The Husband Who Ran Away
A Growing Wonder

With Elizabeth Stevenson Ives:

My Brother Adlai

Beauty Sleep

HILDEGARDE DOLSON

J.B. Lippincott Company
Philadelphia and New York

U.S. Library of Congress Cataloging in Publication Data

Dolson, Hildegarde.
  Beauty sleep.

  I. Title.
PZ3.D6964Be [PS3507.0662]   813'.5'4   76-58517
ISBN 0-397-01209-8

For Dick

Beauty Sleep

1

THE LITTLE FAN whirring in the back room of the Thrift Shop was no more adequate for ventilation than a scrawny bird flapping its wings. The only thing it riffled was the sales chart thumbtacked on the wall directly above the fan and kept up to date by the volunteer who had a firmer grasp of arithmetic than any of the other ladies. She had filled in neatly, with black marking pencil, the weekly and monthly figures on the secondhand merchandise sold for charity; the totals for April, May, June, July had shot up so violently it looked as if the ladies had robbed a bank and added their loot to the take.

The facts were slightly less colorful: Jeanette Eckert, the wealthiest widow in Wingate, Connecticut, had sold her purple elephant of a house with part of the contents, moved to a Florida condominium, and donated her leftovers to the Thrift Shop—the biggest haul in its history. Scatter rugs ranging from Aubusson to yellowish-white bearskin had sold like pizza. The billiard table alone fetched two hundred dollars. A mink coat barely nibbled around the edges caused a nasty confrontation in the back room of the Thrift Shop, volunteer pitted against volunteer, all determined to wear home a bargain. Lucy Ramsdale solved this, as she often solved internecine squabbles when she wasn't causing one herself about politics: "The wide shoulders are tacky. I wouldn't want to see any of you stuck with it." The coat was a size 14; Lucy was a size 10 and didn't like mink anyway. "And everybody in Wingate would know where you got it. Let some pushy type from Danbury have it and pay us a packet." Her argument confused or stunned the other volunteers long enough for her to slap a stiff price tag on the mink and rush it into the display window of the front room, the shop proper, where it had sold almost instantly to the wife of the contractor remodeling the ex-owner's house.

By midsummer, the ladies were nearing the end of the treasure trove, down to the last dozen or so cartons, scraping the barrel almost literally. But what had happened to Jeanette Eckert's thirty-room house plus guest cottages was still a rich source of gossip in the back room of the Second Run Thrift Shop.

That steamy August afternoon, Betsy Green, the youngest volunteer, innocently reprimed the pump. Lucy Ramsdale had described Betsy as "one of the new breed that rise from the sea streaming their hair like mermaids, but they've split their tails to fit into blue jeans."

Betsy's blue jeans were in rugged contrast to the knee-length nylon smocks the other volunteers wore over their dresses. She had recently moved with her husband to Wingate, and now she wanted to know if any of the ladies could recommend a good cleaning woman.

"They're all working at Velanie's Beauty Spa," Liz Carmody said. "You can't even get a plumber if your toilet stops up. They're too busy installing the perfumed Roman baths or whatever at Velanie's. And the prices around here have skyrocketed—carpenter, yardman, the works. God knows Wingate was never cheap, but now it's insane." She ran her plump hand down the front of an angora sweater to make sure all the buttons were anchored, and attached a price tag through a buttonhole. "I suppose it could have been worse, though. A syndicate or something of New York undertakers wanted to buy the whole place and turn it into the Forest Lawn of the East."

Two of her three listeners shuddered pleasurably. The third, Lucy Ramsdale, snorted. For a woman who looked as fragile and exquisite as Meissen china, Lucy had a very strong snort. "I told Jeanette Eckert if she sold to those ghouls she deserved to be their first customer and I'd dance at her funeral."

None of her fellow volunteers questioned this statement. Very few people in Wingate would have questioned it. Lucy had never been twiddle-tongued. She had been a beauty, and she still had the finely whittled bone structure—and sometimes the imperious ways—of a beauty. Recently she'd been involved in investigating several local murders, and unlike those sleuths who believe in keeping their mouths shut, she was still apt to speak her mind. This trait was, at times, the despair of her tenant, Inspector James McDougal, the retired head of homicide of the Connecticut State Police, who lived in the studio behind her house three miles outside Wingate. The studio had been her husband's; Hal Ramsdale had died several years before, and nobody since had been able—or brave enough—to curb Lucy's tongue.

"Where the hell's the dagger?" she said now.

Only the new volunteer, Betsy Green, looked alarmed. The other ladies bent over obligingly to paw through the

11

litter of crumpled newspapers and excelsior on the floor. Liz Carmody came up with the dagger, which had proved to be one of the more useful donations from the Eckert estate, too useful to sell, and handed it over. Lucy grasped the thing by the fake-jewel-encrusted handle and slit open another carton as if it had been a carcass.

"Goddammit, more hollow-stemmed champagne glasses." Lucy and her husband had been well-paid illustrators in the old days in Greenwich Village but they'd never run to hollow-stemmed champagne glasses, and she regarded them as in a class with solid-gold bottle openers, silly examples of Veblen's theory of conspicuous waste. "I thought Jeanette sold most of her china and crystal to the new owner."

"They aren't allowed to drink at the beauty spa," Liz Carmody said. "Only tiger's milk and peppermint tea. Coleman's delivery boy's sister is a maid there, and she told him the rules are terribly strict. One woman brought a bottle of gin—she's a big movie star so you'd think they'd handle her with kid gloves—but Velanie gave her hell and poured the whole bottle into a potted plant right on the spot."

"You can kill a plant that way," Betsy Green said indignantly.

"Well, her new husband certainly drinks. I saw him yesterday in the liquor store. Talk about divine-looking men!" Liz Carmody was a golf widow shaped like an outsize golf ball but without the little holes punched in. "Mr. Fenner told me, 'That's Madame Velanie's husband,' and I swear my nipples stood up and saluted when he passed us. He walks like a prowly tango."

Mary Hunter, a large, placid woman who somehow gave the impression she was sitting in a rocker instead of

12

on a teetery folding chair, said, "Sounds more like a tom-cat."

Liz laughed. "Probably. Coleman's delivery boy's sister said he made a pass at one of the treatment girls, and Velanie fired the girl and practically screamed the house down. She and her husband were in her office with the door closed, but you could hear every name she called him. The only one I remember was 'pig turd.'"

Lucy's nostrils quivered in distaste. She detested scenes—except of her own making. Her temper tantrums, complete with lightning and sound effects, were as short-lived as a summer storm, but while they lasted, strong men had been known to hide under beds.

Liz Carmody was saying, "Of course she has millions, so she can afford to pay alimony. Do you know what a two-ounce jar of her Wrinkles Away cream costs now? Twelve bucks. This new husband looks around thirty-five, so he must have married her for her money. But I give you my word, that man could have had the pick of the field. He's sexier than Valentino."

Mary Hunter took another book from a carton: *How to Find a Pot of Gold in the Stock Market,* published in 1929, and regarded it thoughtfully. Then she plucked a pencil from her firm gray hair and wrote 10¢ in the front.

"You never can tell by looks. I was reading in a magazine just the other day that Rudolph Valentino married two lesbians in a row and the marriages were never consummated."

"Why, that fiend. And women still flinging themselves on his grave."

"Believe me, this husband of Velanie's is not about to bed down with a lesbian."

"Do you suppose Velanie still does it, at her age?"

"With that husband, you'd even do it on your deathbed. Maybe he'll ply her with sex till she dies of exhaustion and then he'll inherit her money. Would that be murder?"

The volunteers looked trustingly at Lucy, who was their self-acknowledged authority on homicide. "I doubt if it would go down as a mercy killing."

"When are you going to bring your inspector to dinner?" Liz Carmody said. "How about Saturday night?"

"He's away. And he's not my inspector. I take his rent and give him fresh linens once a week." This was a chinchy understatement. For one thing, she and Inspector McDougal usually had dinner together. Like most really good cooks, Lucy hated cooking just for herself; and by temperament she needed companionship the way a bird needs wings.

Inspector McDougal wasn't a man to dance attendance, but he had his own way of showing appreciation. He worked like a pitchforking demon in the garden; he bought all the liquor for the ménage; and it was thanks to him that Lucy had been brought into several local murders. Her attitude was that she had drawn him in. The truth was that the understaffed police department in Wingate was pathetically happy to enlist the services of Connecticut's ex-head of homicide. They had more ambivalent feelings about Lucy's services, but they weren't fools enough to tell her, Hands off. It would have been like trying to take candy from a determined baby.

Liz Carmody dived into a crate and hauled out a vaguely Etruscan bas-relief vase or jug at least four feet tall. "Look! A burial urn for Velanie's ashes."

"For God's sake, let's change the subject," Lucy snapped. She ran her hands through her short, curly white hair till it stood out like dandelion fluff. "I'm sick of hearing about that woman."

Liz Carmody obliged with a vengeance. "When will the inspector be back?"

"I haven't the faintest notion. I don't keep tabs on a tenant." This was a big fat fib. Lucy knew exactly how long the police symposium in New York was to last, and McDougal had explained at dinner the night before he left what it was all about: some professor of science had discovered that bullets fired from a gun leave a fallout pattern on the surface below. Police around the country were interested, and wanted to hear more and see demonstrations. The inspector, normally a man who didn't fling words around, much less long sentences, had been downright loquacious on the subject. By the time he reached the metallic residues of antimony and barium, Lucy had been openmouthed—yawning.

Thinking about the inspector's week-long desertion now, she felt resentful and disconnected, as if all her various parts were about to fly off in different directions. She finished polishing two dozen hollow-stemmed champagne glasses with a ragged linen towel, lined them up on an overturned crate, and felt a wicked urge to smash the whole lot with one sweep of her arm.

For timely distraction, Laura Stebble, the cashier and only paid worker, came panting in through the door connecting the shop with the back room. "Guess whose Rolls is in the parking lot."

"If you say Velanie's," Lucy began ominously.

"How did you know? A customer just came in who saw her in the drugstore, and she made the manager change the window display and put all her creams and stuff up front."

15

The only Velanie product Lucy still used was a lipstick. She promised herself to throw it away and buy a Rubinstein lipstick tomorrow.

"What I really came in for," Laura said, "do we have a chamber pot for an avocado pit?"

The older volunteers understood instantly; hand-painted chamber pots had been in big demand all summer as planters, and were now scarcer than mustache cups. The ladies shook their heads regretfully.

"Sell her the burial urn," Lucy said. "Tell her it's a rare find from the Cro-Magnon civilization."

Liz Carmody, having dug up this treasure from a crate, felt possessive. "What if it's really valuable? Maybe the Metropolitan Museum would buy it."

Lucy was in no mood to be argued with. "The Metropolitan has done some silly things lately, but not that silly."

When she left the Thrift Shop soon after four-thirty, she was still so out of sorts that instead of going around the corner to Coleman's Market to pick up something for her dinner, she decided to settle for a poached egg. Jack the butcher, popularly known as Jack the Ripper, had told her he was going to have sweetbreads that Wednesday, and Lucy adored sweetbreads. Inspector McDougal liked the way she did them, with white wine and water chestnuts. But now he had deliberately chosen to stay fifty miles away, in New York, listening to incredibly boring lectures about the metallic residue of bullets. Maybe that was just an excuse. Maybe the real reason he'd gone into New York was to meet his ex-wife, after all that bitch had done to him. The last time she'd summoned him had nearly finished McDougal for good. If I hadn't handled things so delicately, Lucy thought, and got him to sober up and investigate Larry Dilman's death,* Mac might be lying in a gutter right now. This ingratitude on the inspector's part, after the salvation wrought by his selfless landlady, made Lucy so furious she nearly walked past her own car, a Saab, in the parking lot behind the Thrift Shop.

She came to when she heard somebody calling, "Lucy! Lucy Ramsdale!"

Lucy recognized the rather high-pitched voice even before she saw its owner across the parking lot. Adele Woods. In the old days, Hal had called her "hat-head," because she'd always worn teddibly, teddibly chic hats in the office—John Frederics or Lilly Daché—but under the chichi topping a shrewd, lively brain operated at the speed of light. She had been the editor of one of the biggest women's magazines, and she'd never been afraid to plunge in where rivals feared to wet their toes. Lucy remembered her saying, "I've spit into the wind!" That had been the time she'd bought a story about a wife catching syphilis from her husband, which in those days was to invoke the wrath of the gods upstairs—Advertising and Circulation. Hal Ramsdale had done the illustrations; Adele had said, "Lucy's style is too light for this one." But she and her art director had given Lucy plenty of other plums, some of the choicest illustrating jobs around. When you worked for Adele, there was never any niggling about price; she had been as generous with money as she was with praise.

Watching the tall, slim woman in the beautifully cut linen suit walking—almost running—toward her now, Lucy's mercurial spirits soared. It was as if the backwash of the high-riding days had caught her up and carried her to the crest again.

* *Please Omit Funeral.*

17

"Lucy, how marvelous! I could hardly believe my contact lenses."

Adele had to bend to rub cheeks in the ritual greeting of women who don't want to mess their makeup. Seen close to, she was still handsome, but she looked what Lucy thought of as tendonish. Too pulled, as if the muscles were straining like a pole vaulter's.

"Are you here for a weekend?"

Lucy said she'd been living just outside Wingate for twenty years.

"Oh, that house in Connecticut. Of course. I'd forgotten that you and—" She caught herself. "I should have written you when Hal died."

Yes, you should. In a spurt of temper, Lucy said, "Hal would never have recognized you without a hat. He thought you went to bed with a John Frederics on, and a spare on the other pillow."

Adele's laugh was pushed. She put up a hand to smooth her cap of dark hair, which didn't need smoothing: it had the sheen of polished mahogany. "Velanie never wears—" she began, when a bellow erupted.

"Adele! I'm waiting."

"Come on over and meet Velanie." Adele clutched at Lucy's arm. "She's an original. Half peasant—half potentate."

"You're at her beauty spa? My God, I heard it cost fifteen hundred a week."

"I'm hired help. I do publicity."

Oh, my dear, Lucy thought. What happened to bring you down to this? To hide her dismay, she babbled about seeing articles on the spa in every magazine, implying she'd even read them.

Adele's face lit up. "I still have friends in the business.

The editors have been wonderful." With a streak of her old spirit, she added wryly, "Of course the millions Velanie spends on advertising may help a bit, too."

"*Adele!*" The throaty voice was even louder now; the *dele* rang like a gong.

"Please. Come with me."

So she won't bawl you out in front of a stranger? Lucy let herself be hustled along, trying to keep up to Adele's long stride, snatching at scattered, half-remembered bits and pieces. Hadn't Adele married her art director—what was his name?—after they both finally got divorces? They'd been sleeping together long before that and they'd never bothered to hide it. Two of the top people in the business, with the kind of golden sureness that success breeds . . .

Lucy switched her focus to the formidable figure standing beside the Rolls-Royce. Velanie wasn't much taller than Lucy, but so solidly built that from a little distance she had the unyielding look of a stone pillar. Seen from a few feet away, the impression of stoniness vanished. The woman gave off a crackling intensity no photographs of her in ads would ever catch. Eyes as brilliant as black diamonds, played up by a bronze eye makeup that should have looked ludicrous in daylight but somehow seemed right. Magnificent scimitar nose. Licorice-black hair yanked back in a Roman matron's bun. It was a tribute to the powerful face that it made the jewels seem secondary: an enormous ruby and diamond brooch; emerald and ruby rings on three or four of the broad, strong fingers. The woman was making a fist as if she were about to shake it in their faces; her full lips had an ominously sullen set.

I won't let her bully Adele. Lucy gave her best smile, which was very good indeed. "You're one of the few women in the world who doesn't need to be introduced."

Adele was saying "Lucy Ramsdale, an old friend . . ." But the woman seemed not to be listening. She stared at Lucy, then poked a bejeweled finger at Lucy's mouth as if planning to tap a tooth. "Rosy Dawn, eh? Right shade for you. Good."

She had the faintest suggestion of an accent, so that "good" came out more like "goot." "And nice skin, but too dry." The finger moved up and whirligigged around Lucy's right eye. "You should use my creams."

"I used to. But they're too damn expensive for me now."

Velanie chuckled. The sound was unexpectedly rich and warm. "Whatever the traffic will bear, I charge. But mine are the best. I will send you the ones you should have. Adele, write this down. To Mrs. You-know . . ." She rattled off names: "Créme Mesmérique . . . Wrinkles Away . . . Evening Glow . . . Porcelain Peel-Off Mask . . ." It was a lavishly generous list.

Much as Lucy loved presents, her pleasure in this one was soured by the sight of Adele shunted into the role of secretary, meekly making notes on a tiny pad, with, incongruously, an elegant gold pencil.

"How were you ever lucky enough to get Adele? That's like stealing the crown jewels."

Velanie grunted. "She costs me an arm and a foot."

"And worth every—" Lucy nearly said "pound of flesh" but descended to "penny." Adele and that art director husband of hers— The image of him popped up in her mind like a color slide, clearly labeled "Lewis Vining." "Adele, will you give my love to Lewis? How is he?"

Adele dropped her pad and crouched to fumble for it on the concrete. When she straightened up, her mouth was quivering. "Lewis has been very ill. A year ago, he—"

Velanie waved her hands imperiously. "Let's not go into that again. It's a tiresome story." Then, sensing she'd gone too far, she said, "All husbands get tiresome. Mine, too. I've had four—I should know." She smiled at Lucy. "How about you? How many?" The childlike directness kept it from being outrageous.

"One," Lucy said.

"One! For a woman who was beautiful, that's not much."

The past tense stung. "I'll bet mine was worth all of yours put together."

Benign nod. "Perhaps. I married my business young. You stayed home and put your husband first. But I am known all over the world. Millions of women thank me."

"And how many of your husbands thank you?"

Velanie looked as if she'd been bitten on the lip by a butterfly.

Adele Vining said hurriedly, "Lucy and her husband were both well-known artists."

Velanie was diverted. "An artist, eh? I never married an artist, but many famous ones have painted me. My first was an accountant—very useful in the business. Then a banker, also useful. Later a prince who fell off polo ponies once too often. His neck cracked like a chicken bone. And now Jason." She put a wrist up to her face and squinted at a diamond-speckled watch. "He should have been back here by four-thirty. I sent Tompkins to look for him, and now where is Tompkins? Vamoozed." She slapped her hand against the side of the Rolls, so that her rings clunked on the metal. "Both vamoozed. I work day and night and my husband runs loose like a bull."

"You know what you ought to do?" Lucy said. "Chain

Jason on behind the Rolls and drive him through the streets."

Velanie threw back her statuesque head and let out a bark of laughter. "At what speed would you say? Seven miles an hour?"

"Ten or fifteen. Let him pant a little."

"Then throw him to the lions. If the lions ate him up like the ladies do . . ." She rolled her eyes in mock despair.

The two women looked at each other, both glinting with mischief and sudden enjoyment.

"I like you, Loozy. We will be friends. You come see me soon?"

Lucy said she would. "I've been wanting to see what you did with that place."

"I give you a tour, I myself."

Adele said, "Velanie, you've just given me a marvelous idea. Why don't we ask Lucy to come stay at the spa for a week or two and do a series of sketches? I know a half-dozen magazines that would grab them."

Velanie stuck out her lower lip. "But no pay. I give Loozy a week at the spa free, and—"

"But we can't ask her to work for nothing."

Velanie's olive skin turned purplish with rage. "You call fifteen hundred dollars' worth of my treatments and creams nothing? What kind of publicity woman are you?"

Adele Vining said, "Better than you deserve." But she said it under her breath, and her employer's attention had already shifted.

"Loozy, I make you look ten, twenty years younger. Free. You get a hundred percent bargain."

"You'd get a damn good bargain yourself."

Velanie beamed. "It's settled, eh?"

22

"But I can't just leave my"—my what?—"my garden for a week."

A beringed hand brushed this aside. "I send one of my gardeners there. You come tonight, before dinner. Good meals. Lobster, prime beef, caviar—not fattening."

The poached egg on toast at home began to look even flabbier. Lucy hesitated.

"Here's Tompkins now," Adele said. "You can give him directions and he'll pick you up in—what?—say, an hour?"

Lucy protested she'd need time to get her clothes together.

"A toothbrush, nightgown, slippers. Everything else I furnish. Tompkins, where is my husband?"

The chauffeur reminded Lucy of a hound dog in livery. He had large, flapping ears, mournful eyes, and an air of having bayed at the moon too often without results.

"He is coming shortly, Madame Velanie."

"He can walk home."

"With my tail between my legs?" Jason appeared from behind a station wagon as suddenly as a genie.

Lucy, who had pictured a gigolo-ish sort, slinky and heavy-lidded, was surprised to find herself thinking, Hmm, quite a boy. Jason was compactly built, five feet nine or ten, with broad shoulders straining at his sports shirt. Like Velanie, he gave off an immediate high-voltage charge, but of a totally different sort: a bursting physical exuberance. The curly black hair seemed to spring every which way; his eyes, unexpectedly green, sparkled with *goldenwasser* lights. He didn't walk as if he were about to glide into a tango; he walked as if he might leap up a tree after some toothsome prey.

Unlike Liz Carmody, Lucy's nipples didn't stand up and

23

salute, but she responded instinctively to his radiant smile.

Velanie was smiling too, not like a proud mama, but more like a child showing off an incredible new toy, pleased but watchful.

Even Adele was smiling. "Jason, this is Mrs. Ramsdale."

"And I'm Mr. Velanie. Except for Social Security purposes, when I'm known by my maiden name of Pappas." Under the flippant tone, Lucy thought, there was bitterness.

Adele must have heard it too. "Jason was an Olympic diving champion."

"Nice of you to remember. Now I cavort with whales at the spa, and teach them to float under water."

"Very funny. Now we go home to the whales." Velanie turned to get into the Rolls.

"I'm staying awhile. Tompkins plucked me out of the barber's."

Tompkins's mournful eyes flickered as if this were news to him.

More likely a bar without the "ber," Lucy decided. She saw Tompkins's eyes flicker again, this time in the direction of a red Mercedes; an extremely good-looking brunette was just sliding into the driver's seat. Jason put up his hand in what could have been a farewell wave, but as Velanie turned, the hand went instead to his head and he yanked at his curls. "I want to get a haircut."

"No! I pay two fancy-nancy hair stylists at the spa. Use them."

"They're women's hairdressers." He drew himself up, inflated his chest, and beat on it like Tarzan. "Me man."

"Hair's hair. Men are no different from women—above the neck. You will not waste my money."

24

"*Your* money. I earn my measly pay ten times over."

Velanie glared at him and he glared back. The tension between them twanged like a wire.

"Whatever happened to Delilah?" Lucy said. "They don't make them like that any more."

Jason burst out laughing. Velanie's lips twitched at the corners, then stretched into a grin that displayed teeth as perfectly matched as pearls. "She's fun, eh, this Loozy? She's coming to stay at the spa."

Jason's eyebrows inched up, and the quizzical look he gave Lucy was flattering—a why-do-*you*-need-a-beauty-spa? Aloud all he said was "I'm delighted."

"So now you come home with us like a good boy."

The red Mercedes pulled away with one derisive toot of the horn. Jason seemed not to notice; he was suddenly being the attentive husband. "O.K., darling. I'm sorry you had to wait. With three such fascinating women"—his smile encompassed Lucy and Adele, along with his wife— "who could resist their company?"

"Loozy comes later," Velanie said. "Tompkins will pick her up at six."

By six-thirty-five, Lucy was having a first-class fume. She had leaped in and out of a shower, packed an overnight bag, collected her sketch pad, pencils, and paint gear, stowed them in the leather-bound canvas carryall the inspector had given her for her birthday, and decided against a drink because she hated to gulp straight Scotch in a hurry. Now, in her big, uncluttered living room, she sat on the olive-green love seat by the front windows—or, more accurately, quivered there. Waiting, under any conditions, was not compatible with her temperament. Waiting in a welter of second thoughts (why did I fall for this scheme?) was worse. The woman's a monster, she told herself for the third or fourth time. A megalomaniac who thinks she can keep me dangling like the rest of them. Well, she can't. If she thinks she can ply me with tiger's milk and work me like a slave . . .

But, having first renounced the sweetbreads offered by Coleman's butcher, and having set her taste buds on lobster, prime beef, and caviar, it was anticlimactic to fall back on a poached egg. Lucy went to the French doors opening onto the terrace and stared balefully at the bed of giant asters Inspector McDougal had nurtured through drought, beetles, and deer with cloven hooves from the woods behind the studio. If he'd stayed in the studio as he should have, and not gone racing off to explore the metallic fallout of his bitchy ex-wife, then she, Lucy, would be sitting on the terrace with him this minute, having a long, tranquil drink before dinner. Instead of being stuck in this demeaning situation. Velanie only wants me as a pacifier or a Jolly Jester to keep her husband from younger women. How much younger is Jason than Velanie? Hard to tell. He has to be older than he looks, and his wife is as ageless as a Goya. She's bought him, but all her creams and dyes, and her millions, won't keep him in line. And she can't buy *me*. I'll tell her to take her stinking jars and her porcelain mask and . . .

Lucy marched to the phone in the hall by the front door and hauled out the Wingate-Danbury-Ridgefield directory. McDougal had scrawled the number of his New York hotel in the upper left corner of the cover, and she looked at it wistfully, then made herself riffle pages till she found "Velanie's Beauty Spa." The message was already written in her head clear and strong: Please tell Madame Velanie that Mrs. Ramsdale has changed her plans and won't be able to come—ever.

26

Busy signal. Bizzy, bizzy, bizzy. Lucy sat in a storm cloud, waiting to dial again, when she saw, through the screen door, the Rolls advancing sedately, majestically, up her driveway.

Ten minutes later, she was lolling on rosy-red moroccan leather in the back seat of the Rolls, being driven through Wingate's main street. When the car passed Town Hall, which housed police headquarters in its cramped, dingy basement, Lucy looked out the window on that side of the car and thumbed her nose.

Sergeant Terrizi, emerging from the Hungry Bear three doors down with a greasy bag of hamburgers, saw the Rolls and the gesturing occupant, and thought he was having a heatstroke.

2

HAVING DISPOSED of police headquarters—and the inspector *in absentia*—Lucy entertained herself examining the gadgets in the Rolls. The cut-crystal vases on the side panels between window and door each held a single perfect red rose, and she was so intrigued by the scent that she leaned forward to sniff the flower on her side, only to discover it was artificial. Underneath the vase was a miniature gold plaque about the size of an identification disk: "Velanie's Wedding Night." Which wedding? It was hard to picture Velanie humping around making love on the back seat of a car, even a Rolls. Lucy decided it must be the name of a new perfume; she also decided the name would have a limited appeal. Several of her friends who'd been virgins had complained strenuously about their wedding nights. Were any brides virgins now? It seemed unlikely. Probably better this way.

Her attention shifted to the speaking tube, which presumably connected her with Tompkins hermetically sealed away by the thick glass partition. She checked this out after she'd studied a boxlike contraption in place of an armrest on her right. "Tompkins, is this a cassette player?"

Tompkins tilted his rearview mirror to see where his passenger was pointing, then leaned toward the dashboard and declaimed into his end of the speaking tube: "That, madam, is a tape recorder. Madame Velanie often dictates in the car. And in the armrest on the left is a telephone."

It was like an old-fashioned stage direction: *As parlor-maid whisks duster over desk, phone rings.* Tompkins had just finished saying "telephone" when the thing on the left made a noise, although it sounded more like a strangled music box than a phone.

"That will undoubtedly be Madame Velanie. If you lift the—"

Lucy had already edged over on the seat, flipped the lid, and picked up the receiver of a doll-sized phone. "Hello."

"Loozy!" There was nothing strangled about the voice. "Tell Tompkins to stop at the Oags—you know the Oags?"

Lucy, annoyed all over again, said no. The Oags sounded like a tribe of nasty elves.

"The Oags—the inn." Loud and impatient. "He's to pick up my accountant there."

The Oaks! Lucy said all right. She would have liked to complain about having been kept waiting, but the fact that she was talking on a phone in a car inhibited her.

"I have put you in the Jade Empress room, Loozy. North light." The warm, rich chuckle came across full strength. "I know what artists like, eh?"

"Will you feed me on bread and water till I produce?"

The voice rose. "I can't hear you. Bad connection." Bang.

Lucy banged the receiver on her end, and banged the lid for double measure. She decided mutinously she would get out at the Oaks herself, have dinner, and if nobody she knew was there to give her a lift home, she'd order a cab.

29

But when she announced this to Tompkins, after relaying Velanie's instructions to pick up the accountant, the chauffeur's vocal reaction was very unstiff-upper-lip. "Please, madam, she'll have my scalp if I don't bring you along."

Hearing the words over a speaking tube made them seem rather melodramatic, like an SOS at sea.

"Just tell her I didn't like all these delays. It's not your fault I changed my mind."

"That wouldn't matter to the old—" His mutter changed to a near shout. "See, there he is, right in front. Won't take a jiffy."

The man standing on the curb wasn't at all Lucy's idea of an accountant: the one who did her income taxes looked like a cipher with glasses. This man looked more like an old-time matinée idol, complete to the flowing white mane and the flower in the buttonhole. Artificial?

When he hopped spryly into the back seat, it wasn't the flower she smelled; it was whiskey fumes. His heavily veined nose had a W. C. Fields tint. "What an unexpected pleasure." His voice matched the rest of him. "Velanie told me a Mrs. Ramsdale, but she didn't tell me a lovely lady."

Tompkins, standing at attention holding the door, gave Lucy such an imploring look that she nodded and sat back to reassure him. The chauffeur instantly stashed the newcomer's heavy leather bag on the floor in front and hurried around to the driver's seat to start the car before Lucy could change her mind again.

As the Rolls pulled away from the Oaks, Lucy noticed a long red Mercedes in the guests' parking lot next door, and wondered if Jason's good-looking brunette friend was staying there.

Her new companion said, "I'm Arnold Wynn."

Lucy remembered he was an accountant and said something pleasant about what an enormous job it must be to handle Velanie's business affairs.

"I'm related to her, too."

So that explained it—a poor relation.

"Related by marriage. I was her husband for eighteen years." He was pleased with his dragged-in joke. "She turned me in for a banker. And later on, she was able to afford a prince and a string of polo ponies."

"She told me the prince's neck cracked like a chicken bone."

Wynn laughed—the ho-ho-ho of a department-store Santa Claus. "Velanie was always very sentimental. But if she wants to break the new husband's neck—and she will—she'll have to use a meat ax."

"Or empty the swimming pool just before he dives. That might be more practical."

He ho-ho'd again. "Then a client might break her neck. And Velanie would never kill a goose that lays the golden eggs behind the rosy door. That famous rosy-red door. Do you know, when we started the business in three rooms, Velanie bought two cans of paint at Woolworth's and painted the door herself? She wanted to outdo Arden. 'Not pink,' she said. 'Mine is deeper, better.' Even then she had an incredible color sense. And she outdid Arden, all right. I happen to know she's had an offer to sell for thirty-five million."

Lucy made a polite you-don't-say sound.

"When I met Velanie, she was a treatment girl at Arden's and I had my own accounting firm. Finally I had to give it up because Velanie's business got so big it needed all my time. You know how much stock I own in Velanie?"

Lucy shook her head. All this man needed was a robot

to converse with. If he said, Guess how many shares, she'd kick him.

"None! Velanie bought me out one time when I owed a few thousand to a— Well, never mind. I won't bore you with my troubles."

Lucy had always disliked people who said, "I won't bore you with my troubles." If they were stupid enough to say it, they deserved an answer of "No, don't." But she'd never yet said it out loud, and Wynn was no person to start on. Besides, she was curious. She said she'd only met Velanie that afternoon. "I remember way back there was some ridiculous publicity story about her being the illegitimate daughter of Queen Marie of Rumania, and inheriting the royal beauty secrets."

This time, the ho-ho ended in hiccups, but Wynn was too wound up to stop talking. "She was Rumanian, all right. Hic. Legitimate daughter of a peasant. Hic. She got the formula for the first cream from an uncle who was the village apothecary. Then she lit out and went to—hic—pardon me." The hiccups were coming faster. He used the handkerchief that had been pointing nattily out of his breast pocket to wipe his streaming eyes. In a wheezing tone, he said, "Need a drink. Brought a flask. Medicinal."

Lucy was amused by the word. "I brought a flask, too, but it's not medicinal. I like a drink before dinner, and from what I'd heard of the spa, they tipple on peppermint tea."

"Or molasses in warm milk. Horrible thought. Scotch O.K. with you?"

Lucy said Scotch was fine. She almost added, Hic. "But why don't I drink my own so you won't run short?"

"Have a full bottle in my bag. Hic."

Wynn's pocket flask was gold, or at least a glistening facsimile. He unscrewed the jigger top and filled it with a surprisingly steady hand. "You drink out of this. More where that came from. Cheers." He tilted his head back, put the flask to his lips, and his Adam's apple seemed to leap to the treat.

While his right arm was raised, Lucy noticed his shirt cuff was slightly frayed, and averted her eyes out of tact. "Cheers." She sipped cautiously from the jigger; it wasn't very good Scotch. Inspector McDougal had conditioned her to better.

Wynn finally lowered the flask. "Velanie gave me this, one Christmas soon after we were married. I found out later a dealer had given it to *her*, but at the time I was deeply touched by her generosity." His inflection put the last word in heavy-hanging quotes. Either the whiskey or the thought of Velanie's "generosity" seemed to have stopped his hiccups. "You should have seen her in those days. Beautiful girl. Incredibly striking."

Lucy said she thought Velanie was still very striking, and mentioned the likeness to Goya.

"A Goya trying to be a *goy*. She should have stuck to her own race when she married again."

"What a stupid thing to say." Lucy sat up so straight she spilled some of her whiskey. "Here, take this damn thing." Even to her it sounded harsh, and she tried to soften it. "I can't drink and drive."

Her companion took the jigger and drained the rest of the Scotch in one gulp. "Didn't mean that the way you thought. But Jews aren't gigolos."

Even while she shrugged off the generality, she found herself thinking with surprise, He may be right. "You make Jason sound like a beachboy. He was an Olympic star."

33

"That's not a profession."

"A flash in the pool?" She was miffed that Wynn didn't even smile.

"He was a swimming coach in a New York gym when she found him."

"Don't tell me Velanie was trotting over to a gym to practice her crawl."

"Not her. She was hiring staff for the spa. And when she saw that Greek water-baby, she wanted him for keeps. My God, do you know how much older she is than—" He broke off and looked so rattled Lucy couldn't imagine what had hit him.

He was fumbling with the gadget on his right, checking something.

"Whew! Forgot the tape recorder. It's off, all right. Velanie puts it on when she wants to hear what somebody's saying behind her back. She caught me once that way, with a—shall I say a female companion?"

Was the companion medicinal too? Lucy wondered.

"That was bad enough. But if she heard me telling you how old she is she'd slit my belly. Nobody knows but me." He wanted to be coaxed; Lucy was mildly curious, but she wouldn't play roguish games.

"I assumed Jason was quite a bit younger. But that's nothing these days. It's the trend. And I find it a pleasant switch from old men panting after nubile maidens."

To her surprise, Wynn turned a blotchy red. "Not the same thing," he muttered. "This obsession of Velanie's is—well, dangerous. Thing is, Jason bucked her. Didn't act interested."

"That doesn't sound like a gigolo."

"He was only playing hard to get. So she had to have him. Reminded me of a time in South America years ago.

34

We'd gone down there to see about opening up some new branches. Velanie picked up a baby jaguar—beautiful little beast—and wanted to take it home as a pet. And she bribed enough people to get it on the plane with us. When we got back to New York, she even let it sleep on her bed. All very cuddly. But the cub grew up in a hurry. Jumped at me one day and clawed the hell out of my chest. Thirty stitches." He was pawing his shirtfront, and for one awful second Lucy thought he was going to show her his scars. But he seemed satisfied just to have pinpointed the location. "Velanie said I'd brought it on myself by being hostile. But when the animal turned on her—a claw just grazed her cheek—she wanted to have it shot. Finally she gave it to a zoo."

"Well, she can't give Jason to a zoo. Or even have him shot."

"You'd be surprised what she can do. After all the years I'd slaved for that business—helped her build it up from a few piddling jars of glop to a worldwide corporation—and then she threw me out like some little stock boy. Got in a bunch of young Wharton Business School graduates who know how to run a computer."

"Button, button, who'll punch the button?"

Wynn ignored the remark; he seemed incapable of listening, and Lucy was used to being listened to. She thought her button-button line deserved better; it could be the theme song of the nuclear age. Inspector McDougal would have appreciated it. In a burst of honesty, she thought, No, Mac wouldn't have paid any attention. He doesn't like flip remarks. But when I'm around him, I don't have to rattle like ice at a cocktail party. She glanced out her window and sighed when she saw they had another mile or so to go.

35

". . . put me on a retainer as a consultant, less than she pays a gardener. But now that the conglomerate's made her this offer, it's not the boy graduates she turns to—it's me, Arnold Wynn. I know more about that business than anybody alive or dead. So she'll 'pay my expenses' if I come up here and go over some figures with her. That's a good one—'pay my expenses'! I reserved a room at the Oaks; then I find a message when I arrive saying, 'Call Madame Velanie—urgent!' You know what was so urgent? She didn't see why I should waste forty dollars a night on a room when she had plenty of rooms at the spa. So I say all right, I'll take a cab and go right out there, but that's an even bigger squawk—'a crazy waste of her money.' Tompkins is picking up somebody in Wingate and I'm to wait in the lobby at the Oaks till the car comes. 'Not in the bar,' she tells me. 'You're no good to me drunk.' So I go into Ye Olde Taproom and I charge two doubles to Madame Velanie." He looked at Lucy—really looked—and smiled wryly, and she saw a flash of the charm he must have had once. "The truth is I didn't enjoy a drop of it. All those phony oak beams eaten by phony worms, and ye olde warming pans hanging all over the place. And no pretty lady to talk to. I'm glad now that Velanie wouldn't pay for a cab." Doffing of the imaginary hat again. "This your first visit here?"

Lucy said crisply she had agreed to do some sketches of the place.

"Nail her to a contract. Get the price down in writing. She hates to put anything on paper, but stick to your guns."

Lucy had no intention of telling him the embarrassing truth: that she wasn't to be paid a cent. She said everything was already satisfactorily arranged.

36

Wynn was shrewder than he looked. "Held out the bait of a free stay at the spa, didn't she, in return for your working your ass off? Pardon the language, but when I'm on the subject of Velanie and money—she doesn't just pinch a penny till the eagle screams, she wrings the bird's neck and picks the carcass. Then she'll go off and spend a few hundred grand for one ring." He laughed, not the ho-ho-ho, but a natural, pleasant sound. "You have to hand it to the old girl, though. Know what she did when a burglar got into her bedroom in the New York house? He wanted the combination to the wall safe where she keeps her jewels, and he was waving his gun around—'Give it to me or I'll shoot.' And Velanie told him, 'Shoot me, then. I'm an old woman. I might die any minute anyway.' Only time in her life she ever called herself an old woman, that's for sure. It was lucky she pulled it on a professional thief and not some trigger-happy junkie. The guy was so rattled he just turned and ran." Wynn was sounding quite fatuous. "When all's said and done, there's nobody like Velanie."

"Thank God," Lucy muttered.

To her relief, the car turned in between stone pillars connected overhead by an arching sign in rosy-red letters: VELANIE'S BEAUTY SPA.

Wynn was still on the burglar. "Good thing he didn't shoot her. She hadn't even made a will." The fatuous note had gone. "I'll tell you confidentially— Well, look who's blowing kisses! Miss Ice Chest herself." He was staring past Lucy, out her window, and she turned to look. At first, all she could see were several life-size statues—the barefoot draped-lady sort—in an elaborately landscaped garden. But then a figure appeared from behind one of the statues— and what a figure. The girl was in shorts, and she had legs no statue could ever compete with. Her probable bust measurement, in a sleeveless jersey, made the title Miss Ice Chest singularly inappropriate. She wasn't blowing kisses now; she was walking quickly toward what looked like a bubble-domed swimming pool.

"I take it that's not a 'client,' " Lucy said. "Or if she is, she's a spectacular advertisement for 'After Velanie got through with me.' "

"Client! Celia Grant a client! She rides herd on 'em. Came to work in the New York salon as a kid, a stockroom girl. Velanie took a fancy to her and had her trained in the cosmetics end at our Long Island plant. Went on the road selling creams, giving demonstrations in stores. Worked her way up to be manager of the New York salon. Now she runs the spa."

"She doesn't look old enough."

"Must be around thirty-five. And I'd have bet she never—uh—" While he groped for a word with more than four letters, Lucy supplied the right active verb in her mind and stayed demurely silent. "Uh—tumbled in the clover."

It had a pleasanter sound than "rolled in the hay," which had always sounded scratchy to Lucy, more fitting for moo-cows.

"Coldest piece of young flesh I ever met." While he watched the girl, he was wetting his lips. "Heard that over and over from the salesmen."

After you'd already checked it yourself. Lucy was studying him—the wet lips, the glistening bloodshot eyes— when she caught a glimpse of movement through the window on his side. A man's head popped up behind a box-wood hedge, then ducked almost instantly, but not before Lucy's artist's eye had registered a vivid impression.

Wynn was talking more to himself. "Now who the hell was she blowing kisses to?"

Lucy thought she knew.

"Something tells me it wasn't a pansy hairdresser or the chef. And the rest of the staff here is female, all but—" He was staring straight ahead now, at Tompkins's neck, and still talking more to himself. "Not that I begrudge her having a little fun, but if it's fun with who I think it is, she's playing with more than his— I mean, she's playing with dynamite."

"Or eating the candle at both ends," Lucy said.

3

When Inspector McDougal got back to his hotel room at seven, the message light on the phone by the bed was not only flashing; it was emitting an *eek, eek, eek* of distress. The inspector was a long-legged man and he covered the space between the door and the phone in approximately two seconds. Lucy. Lucy must have been trying to reach him. She wouldn't have called just to chitchat. Had to be something important. He was already dialing the desk. "McDougal in room seven fourteen. You have a message for me."

"Oh, yes, Mr. McDougal, just a moment. . . . *Inspector* McDougal. You are to call Inspector Hanson in Hartford, Connecticut. He will be at the state police headquarters awaiting your call, and the number is—"

"I know the number." He could hardly bring himself to say thank you to a creature who had given him a message he didn't want and withheld the message he might have had from Lucy. Probably Hanson had changed his mind and wanted to come down for at least part of the police conference.

"Inspector Hanson said it was urgent."

Urgent. That was different. Lucy hadn't been able to reach him at the hotel and had left a message for him with the state police.

His old colleague in homicide, now Inspector Hanson, was maddeningly genial. "Mac, it's good to talk to you. How are things down there?"

"Hot as hell. Did Lucy Ramsdale call you?"

Hanson sounded surprised. "No. Why?"

McDougal began to feel silly. Why indeed? If Lucy had wanted to reach him through the police, why not the Wingate police?

"She involved in another bloodletting?"

Ordinarily, James McDougal was an almost painfully honest man, a descendant of painfully honest Scots, but now he did a slight Highland fling around the truth: "It looked as if something might break there soon, and I've been out of touch."

"This is the season for things breaking, all right. We've had two nice, simple, record-heat killings today. Husbands drank their weight in beer to cool off, then got into what Patrolman Murphy describes in his report as 'a heated argument with wife.' One dame sliced like a meat loaf. The other shot in the head. Saturday-night special pushed up to Wednesday. Husband couldn't wait to tell us all about it—sobbing and sudsing. No need for a fancy ballistics test on this one. How does the new theory—that metallic residue stuff—hold up in demonstrations?"

McDougal said it had possibilities.

"Good. A fallout pattern on bullets would be a damn sight more help as evidence in court than neutron activation."

McDougal thought Hanson was being untypically chatty; he wondered why. While his ex-colleague talked on, his glance wandered to a brochure beside the phone, emblazoned in blood red: HAVE YOURSELF A SWINGING TIME IN OUR SWING-HIGH LOUNGE. ENTERTAINMENT BY THE FAMOUS ROCK SPLITTERS.

McDougal's long, bony face became even more dour as he contemplated this horror. He almost missed what Hanson was saying:

". . . hate to tell you like this but I thought you ought to know."

"Know what?" But even as he said it, he had a sickening sense of what was coming: something to do with Eileen. It was Hanson who had told him finally, reluctantly, what half of Hartford already knew—that his wife was sleeping with another man. McDougal had handed in his resignation that same week, recommended Hanson to take his place as head of homicide, and left Hartford abruptly.

"Your ex-wife's back in town. She divorced that guy Torrance."

"I heard she was going to." McDougal's lips felt stiff, as if the Novocain hadn't worn off. "But you needn't worry. I have no intention of seeing her."

"What I really wanted to tell you"—Hanson cleared his throat—"I'm afraid she has every intention of seeing you. She said she'd heard you were 'living with some woman' and it had 'whetted her appetite,' so she wants to break it up."

"There's nothing to break up." But he was so angry he trembled. "Lucy Ramsdale is my landlady."

"Who turns up corpses to keep you from getting rusty. If she's turned up a new one, I'd better send Detective Carlin down to work with you again. He still talks about 'the cute little lady who found the body in the clothes bin.' * He'd leap at the chance to come."

* *To Spite Her Face.*

42

McDougal had a sudden picture of Detective Carlin, with his mournful eyes ringed like a raccoon's, padding into Wingate police headquarters to aid in a nonexistent murder case. He said quickly, "Nothing concrete has developed yet."

"If Eileen tackles Lucy Ramsdale, you may have something concrete anyway—like a catfight with no claws barred."

"Lucy wouldn't have any part of that. And, to be fair, it doesn't sound like Eileen either."

"Eileen's drinking quite a bit. Tears around in a red Mercedes. Already picked up twice for speeding. Is there anything you'd like me to do at this end? Short of locking her up for being a private nuisance? Her family's still pretty big stuff around here. Her brother's running for governor."

"Is she staying with him?"

"She was. But I suspect she's not exactly good for the candidate's image. Eileen moved into the Mansford Hotel."

"I'll call her there and put an end to this nonsense."

"Mmm." Hanson's doubt hummed over the line. "Sorry I had to break the news to you over the phone, but I couldn't get down there to join you. We have two men on vacation."

"It's time you took a vacation of your own."

Hanson said, "How many real vacations did you take in the fifteen years you had this job?"

As McDougal hung up, his mind was back in a variation of the rat maze he'd wandered in endlessly when he'd first come to Wingate: If I'd taken more real vacations . . . If I'd spent more time with Eileen . . . She used to say I never wanted to go anyplace unless I was promised an interesting corpse. . . .

He took off his gray Dacron summer jacket and hung it up automatically, then pulled off his tie. With the tie in his hand, he focused on it, finally, and the rat maze evaporated. Lucy had bought it for him at the Thrift Shop. As she'd said at the time, "Where else could you get a practically new Countess Mara tie for a quarter?" It was a scrawled pattern of white M's on dark blue, and it was still a good-looking tie. "I know you hate things initialed," Lucy had said. "But the M is for mayhem."

Today would have been Lucy's afternoon at the Thrift Shop. She'd be home by now. Probably having a drink on the terrace right this minute. Allow time for her to get indoors to the phone. Should he mention Eileen? No. No point in getting Lucy stirred up over something that wouldn't happen. Better call Eileen in Hartford first, and make it clear once and for all that he was through. Would she still be using the name of Torrance?

She was. But Eileen Torrance had checked out of the hotel at 2 P.M. No forwarding address. What if she'd gone straight to Wingate?

When he dialed Lucy's number, he pictured her, on the first four rings, putting down her Scotch and water, banging the screen door as she went in through the French doors, and walking quickly to the phone in the hall. On the next four rings, he let her get out of the shower, cursing, dripping, and reach her bedside extension. After six more rings, he gave up and lit a cigarette that tasted like rusty brass. He had spent all day at lectures and demonstrations, and he'd already smoked a pack and a half. Better have a drink and some dinner and try Lucy again later.

By twenty minutes after eleven, after a dozen more futile tries, he was so worried he called the Wingate police.

"Mrs. Ramsdale's not home," Sergeant Terrizi said

44

helpfully. "I saw her going by in a Rolls around seven."
He tactfully didn't mention Lucy's thumb-to-nose salute as
the Rolls passed police headquarters. "I recognized the
car—it belongs to Velanie's Beauty Spa. But when I saw
who was in the back seat, I thought at first I was seeing
things."

"You were," the inspector said. "Lucy wouldn't be
caught dead in a beauty spa."

"Well, she wasn't dead at nine tonight. Mama was filling in at the spa for my cousin, and she saw Mrs. Ramsdale there at dinner. Listen, do you know a good-looking
brunette name of Torrance?"

McDougal sounded as if he were choking on a wish-
bone; he managed to croak, "Yes."

"Well, she came into headquarters wanting to get in
touch with you. Said it was personal. Bayles was on the
desk and he told her he couldn't give out any information.
So then she sees Chief Salter and wangles it out of him
that you're away all this week."

"He should have said for a year. If you see her again—"

"Somebody saw her in that bar next to the barbershop
this afternoon with Velanie's husband. He teaches swimming or something out at the spa. The two of them were
getting pretty cozy when the chauffeur came and broke it
up."

McDougal felt as if he were growing two heads. His ex-
wife had always had money of her own, but she'd always
driven herself. Maybe now that she was drinking too much
. . . "You mean Eileen's chauffeur?"

"Who's Eileen?"

"Mrs. Torrance." McDougal was beyond explaining in
more detail. He could almost hear the wheels turning in
Terrizi's cerebellum as the sergeant digested this.

45

"Oh, the brunette. No, it's Madame Velanie's chauffeur. Same one that drove Mrs. Ramsdale out to the spa."

"Lucy was probably going there to have dinner with some friend."

"No. She's staying awhile. Mama saw her later in her room. And I grant you Mama's got a wild imagination, but it's not *that* wild."

4

THE MAIN HOUSE was designed in a style of architecture Lucy had once called Gothic Colonial. The white pillars traditional to New England (even Wingate's supermarket had pillars) flanked an entrance complete with fanlight. And above, turrets, towers, and other excrescences abounded.

The only outside change Lucy noticed was the color of the door, painted a rosy red—Velanie's trademark. Inside, the change was eye-popping. What had been a long, gloomy, walnut-paneled main hall was prettified beyond recognition. The wood paneling was now painted glistening white; the upper wall was emerald green, with a design of long-stemmed red roses flung seemingly at random. Even the ceiling was agog with roses. And the newel-post at the foot of the staircase, which had once supported a hefty bronze maiden clutching a torch, had a pot of red roses squatting on top.

There was certainly no rosy-red carpet rolled out for the new arrivals. The hall was empty. Tompkins put down their bags near the door. "They're serving dinner in the staff dining room in the other building. So if there's nothing more you'd like, madam—" He was halfway out the door when he added, "Miss Grant should be along any minute."

"If she's not too busy throwing kisses around," Arnold Wynn muttered.

Lucy had had more than enough of his company, and she resented being left here to cool her heels. "Tell them I've gone for a walk," she said, and went out even faster than Tompkins.

The only trouble with this excuse was that she was wearing her best Ferragamo pumps, size 4, and they were definitely not designed for walking, especially on the pebbly path that led toward the enclosed swimming pool. She had low-heeled shoes in her overnight case, but to go back and change shoes in the hall meant being stuck with Wynn again. As a concession to her expensive pumps, she sat down on an iron bench so implacable it made her rear end feel ridged like a waffle. In exasperation, she yanked off her shoes and leaped onto the grass, which felt deliciously, greenly cool on her stockinged feet. Pumps in hand, she wandered for five or ten minutes, past the long, glass-domed pool—empty—past the tennis court—empty, but with a superbly graceful hawthorn tree just beyond. Sketch two players in a singles match, with the tree for background. She stood there studying the hawthorn, and as the drawing took shape in her mind, she felt soothed, even peaceful. Lithe, small players . . . their outfits in a clear yellow . . . But as she pictured these graceful creatures, she suddenly remembered where she was—in effect, a reducing spa—and burst out laughing. Well, slim them down for sweet publicity's sake—or, rather, for Adele's sake. Odd that Adele hadn't been around to welcome her.

Maybe she was eating now in the staff dining room. Lucy began to feel sharply hungry. It was almost seven-thirty.

When she got back to the house, shod again, she was annoyed to see Arnold Wynn there, alone. He was sitting on a rosy velvet-upholstered settee beside his suitcase, staring straight ahead. For some reason, his head was moving back and forth like a spectator's at a tennis match, but instead of turning, it was rocking, left, right, left, right.

Lucy had hoped to avoid him, but she was so baffled by his head motions that she walked over to see what had struck him.

"Take a look," he murmured, and moved over on the settee so that Lucy could have a vantage point. She was now looking into the half-open door of what seemed to be a cardroom and lounge. Five women wearing identical pale pink brocade pants suits sat in front of a massive color television set, watching the screen intently. What made it somewhat unusual was that they were sitting on the floor, legs drawn up to chins, hands clenched around their knees, and rocking back and forth, back and forth, on their sizable buttocks.

"I'm getting seasick," Wynn complained.

A door at the far end of the hall swung open and Celia Grant hurried toward them. "Oh, Mrs. Ramsdale, I do hope you haven't been waiting long."

"No, but Mr. Wynn has."

Celia nodded to him coolly. Seen close to, her figure was even more spectacular, but her features had that exquisitely monotonous regularity of a mannequin's. The wide eyes were too pallid a blue, and the smile on her lips went just so far and no farther.

Too tepid for heaven or hell, Lucy said to herself, carelessly misquoting Dante.

Celia Grant's voice had a measured-out sweetness, and for Lucy the measure was fulsome. "We're so delighted to have you with us. Madame Velanie is tied up on a call to Paris, so she asked me to take you to your room and she'll see you at dinner in her cottage."

Wynn said, "Good. Then maybe we can wangle a drink there."

Celia Grant's smile tightened. When she spoke again, a frosty vapor seemed to encircle each word: "Madame will see you *after* dinner, Mr. Wynn. If you want to unpack now, your quarters are in the stable."

"The stable—Christ!"

"Madame had it all remodeled, and most of the staff live there. It's the long building to the left behind the house, and the staff dining room is still open, so if you hurry . . ."

Wynn made a feeble effort at saving face. He said to Lucy, "Now you see what I mean about Velanie's stinginess. The stable and leftovers for the hired help."

The girl caught fire then. "Velanie is the most generous person ever. If you knew all the people she's helped—and you should. You're one of them. Bailing you out over and over—" She caught herself. "I beg your pardon, Mrs. Ramsdale, but I just couldn't bear to have you get a false impression of Velanie. Ask your friend Mrs. Vining— *she'll* tell you. And now let me show you your room. It's one of our loveliest." She picked up Lucy's carryall and overnight bag. "Aren't you clever to travel light! I always think that takes such character."

Her glance flicked over Wynn's outsize leather suitcase. "Madame will see you at nine-fifteen sharp, in her office. I suggest you get plenty of black coffee with dinner."

Wynn reached down for his bag, and Lucy saw the

frayed cuff again. In one of her mercurial shifts, she forgot she'd rather disliked him. Now he was an underdog who'd been kicked in her presence, and she wouldn't put up with it.

"I think I'll have dinner in my room. Mr. Wynn, won't you join me? I hate to eat alone. Please."

It was touching to see him revive. And gratifying to see Celia Grant flustered. "But Madame Velanie wouldn't— she'd be terribly put out. It's really out of the question."

Lucy was pleased that her ploy had worked; she moved into Phase 2: "Then why don't Mr. Wynn and I both join Velanie for dinner?"

"But I'll have to consult her—I can't interrupt her Paris call. She planned just the threesome—you and her husband, Mr. Pappas, and herself."

Wynn said abruptly, "I don't want to eat with Pappas. I'd tell the fella to his face what I think of him. By the way, have you got another new man on the staff?"

Celia shook her head.

"That's funny. When we turned in to the driveway tonight, I saw you blowing kisses like crazy. There was no car around, so I figured it had to be somebody on the staff."

Just for a second, the girl's face went blank with shock. If Lucy hadn't been watching closely, she'd have missed it.

"Oh, my stepbrother! Of course. He's interning at Norwalk Hospital and he came over to see me. A friend dropped him off here, and was picking him up."

It was done so smoothly Lucy was almost convinced herself.

"I thought Velanie told me way back you were an orphan."

"I am. What a marvelous memory you have, Mr.

Wynn. Raymond and I were both farmed out to foster parents, and we lost track of each other for years. It was like a miracle to run into him in Norwalk."

Wynn looked rather confused but quiescent.

"I'd hoped so much he'd stay and have dinner with me, but he had to go back on duty. Mr. Wynn, why don't *you* have dinner with me?" She clasped her hands girlishly. "Would you?"

Wynn was oozing gratification, with two women wanting him at once.

"Would you mind?" he asked Lucy, who kept a straight face and said, "Of course not."

"I'll just go over and freshen up first."

As Wynn started off with his bag, he lurched and nearly banged into the rose-spotted wall.

You said you had a bottle with you, Lucy thought. More like four quarts.

Wynn had recovered his balance and was making his farewells jauntily. "Another evening, dear lady," he said to Lucy, with revolting roguishness.

At the front door, he blew a kiss to Celia. "I'll be along in two shakes of a ram's tail."

Lucy could see the girl flinch and almost felt sorry for her. But Celia was instantly in command of herself, projecting an image of poised hostess. "Sorry about the tiresome delay. I do hope you'll like your room."

As Lucy got up, she glanced across the hall again, into the lounge, where the five women were still in dogged motion. "What the hell are they doing?"

"Oh, rocking away their TV bottoms. Miss Tringle, our directress of the exercise program, won't let them watch otherwise. She won't even allow TV sets in their rooms. At home, they sit for hours just looking, and their buttocks positively expand." She went to the door of the lounge and called, "Aren't you good girls! Miss Tringle will bring your drinks when she comes back from dinner."

"Molasses in warm milk?" Lucy said.

"Tonight it's crab-apple juice. When Madame took me to a very famous spa in Switzerland, we were on an apple diet for days. Whole or grated or juice. And of course there's Bircher-Brenner's fabulous apple muesli. All terribly good for high blood pressure. The Swiss are so advanced on health matters. Did Mrs. Vining tell you about the trip Velanie is giving her, to a remarkable new clinic in Zurich?"

"Why should Adele go to a clinic?"

"For her husband. A doctor there is experimenting with a new treatment for lateral sclerosis—you know, the disease her husband has."

Lucy let out a little moan. She'd had a favorite friend die, too slowly, of this same thing. Poor Lewis. Poor Adele.

"Mrs. Vining had to go over to the nursing home in Danbury tonight because her husband was worse." Celia Grant was saying all this in the same chatty tone as she shepherded Lucy down the hall. "But it's done her so much good to know they'll soon leave for Switzerland. She was sorry not to be here to welcome you. Oh, and Madame said to tell you not to bother changing. We do have the clients dress for dinner—they eat at six because that's better for their diets—Pierre Cardin evening suits . . . lovely Chinese silks . . . so important for morale. But tonight you'll be dining *en famille*. Madame took such a fancy to you."

The beautiful long legs were moving so fast that Lucy, who was five or six inches shorter than the girl, felt hustled. When they reached the end of the long hall, she stopped, rebelliously, to examine a portrait of Velanie. She knew it was a Walling even before she saw the signature. "I used to know the painter."

"Oh, how nice. If you'd like to sit here for a moment to admire it, I'll go over to Madame's office and make sure her secretary has all the figures ready for the meeting. It's just around the corner."

Lucy sat on another of the rosy-red velvet settees across from the painting and sneered at it. She and Hal had known Walling in the old days in the Village, when he'd been so broke he did portraits of out-of-town suckers at five dollars a head, at the outdoor art show. Eventually he'd opened a studio on Fifty-seventh Street and graduated from out-of-town suckers to New Yorkers who wanted to be done in oil, with their finery painted in excruciatingly photographic detail, and their features remade to best advantage.

This portrait had to be of a much younger Velanie, but all Walling's sitters dropped at least twenty years on canvas. He had bobbed the magnificent scimitar nose, and made the eyes as expressive as a dead fish. But he had rendered full homage to the elaborate ruby necklace and rings.

"Loozy!"

To see Velanie in the vital flesh standing under the flaccid facsimile was invigorating. "You like it?" She waved a beringed hand at the portrait.

"The jewelry's well done."

Velanie chuckled. "I made him do over the rubies six times. He was ready to stab me here—" she clasped her commanding bosom—"with a palette knife."

"If you try to make me do over a sketch even once, I'll do worse than that."

54

"I'm not such a fool. The way I know how to pick colors, I know how to size up people."

But not husbands, Lucy thought as Celia reappeared.

"Take this child." Velanie patted Celia's pretty bare arm. "You should have seen her when she came to work for me. Frizzy hair, ten-cent lipstick, scared like a rabbit."

In Lucy's experience as a gardener, rabbits were considerably bolder than wolves, which made Velanie's comparison even more interesting.

"Only I, Velanie, could spot what was underneath. She had drive, this child, and brains. And she grabbed at a chance to learn."

"I owe everything to Madame. She's been like a"—the "child" knew better than to say "a mother"—"like a big sister and fairy godmother to me."

"Godmother" was safe, implying no age, merely a wand-waving miracle worker.

Velanie obviously agreed with this assessment; her head went up and down like a mandarin's. "But she repays me, this child. The business, my problems, my worries—these are her life."

Lucy, watching Celia's face express selfless devotion, gratitude, dedicated loyalty, remembered an old line of Dorothy Parker's about an actress emoting on stage: "She ran the gamut from A to B." But considering the kisses thrown to Jason Pappas earlier, it wasn't a bad job of acting.

Velanie, sensing she'd lost her guest's attention, yanked the spotlight back to herself. "You think this portrait doesn't do me justice, eh? Only the jewels look real?"

Lucy smiled and nodded.

Celia made a little cry of protest. "Oh, no! I think the whole painting is marvelous."

55

"You know nothing about painting." Velanie's tone was as brusque as a shove. "Loozy does. She is right."

To Lucy, she said, "The painter—Walling—married a Rumanian girl from my village. Beautiful but stupid. She got pregnant—they needed money. So I let him paint me. Then he could say to all the rich ladies, 'See how fine I am. Even Madame Velanie commissions me.' And they rushed to sit for him. Pah. Sheep. Someday I show you the Grant Sutherland portrait of me in my town house. *Belle laide.* Cost twenty times this smear of Walling's. The jewels—a nothing, but in that one *I* am real. And the Picasso sketch. You know how he did my ruby necklace? A black squiggle like a little garter snake around my neck."

She saw that Lucy was charmed and amused. "What a man! Strong as an ox. In his studio, he had six canvases on six easels, and he'd go from one to the other. He could work all night, like me. And he knew food, like me. His cook used to make a bouillabaisse"—Velanie put her hand to her lips and made a smacking sound—"with even the same delicate rock crab they have only in Marseilles bouillabaisse—the best. My chef here is as good. I brought him from France. You will see tonight."

Lucy said, "The sooner the better. Your chauffeur was late and then we had to stop to pick up Mr. Wynn."

"Was Arnold souzzled?"

"What a good word." Lucy sidestepped the question fast, but not very effectively. "Souzzled. I must remember it."

Velanie wasn't diverted; she scowled so hard the brilliant eyes were shut down to slits. "Celia, tell Tompkins to go through the luggage while Arnold's eating, and take any bottles. Probably too late already."

Celia said, "I'm having dinner with Mr. Wynn in the

staff dining room, so I can get him sobered up with black coffee before your meeting."

And fuddle him more about your mythical stepbrother Raymond. Aloud, Lucy said, "I could use a drink myself."

"I ordered champagne for dinner," Velanie said expansively. "Celia, go take care of Arnold. I show Loozy her room."

The room, at the back of the main floor in the corner, was about the size of Lucy's bedroom at home, but considerably fancier: a jade-colored satin spread on the queen-size bed, with a matching phone on the night table. The dressing table had a three-way mirror edged in theater-makeup lights, and as Velanie was quick to point out, the top was already loaded with jars and bottles of the products she'd recommended for Lucy: "All free, and I give you more to take home. This peel-off porcelain mask—fantastic. You must try it tonight. Come, I show you your terrace." She pulled back the floor-length curtains that covered most of the rear wall—green with the ubiquitous roses—and opened a glass-paneled door. "Good north light when you want to paint here." Along with several pieces of wrought-iron terrace furniture, there was a draftsman's table she pounded approvingly. "Solid—for your work. I think of everything, eh, Loozy? Now we go eat. If you want to go to bathroom first, three in my cottage."

Her so-called cottage, directly behind the main house, was a large stone house that had been known as "the party place" in the ex-owner's day. The forty-foot-long main room had often been used for dancing, with a raised section, three steps up, at the far end, where a five-piece band had played. That now seemed to be a dining area, with a kitchen opening off it. Lucy remembered there were several bedrooms upstairs.

Either the party room had shrunk or it was so over-stuffed it bulged at the seams. There were two gilt settees, perhaps relics of an early Madame Velanie salon, along with high-backed black-walnut chairs, squashy old sofas, teetery small tables piled with objets d'art, everything from a bronze Buddha morosely contemplating his navel to a gaudy ceramic figure of a flamenco dancer. Lucy spotted a Dufy hanging next to an atrocious landscape with cows, and was reminded of an auction room: the junk and the treasures cheek by jowl.

"Welcome to the witch's gingerbread cottage," Jason said. He was leaning over the iron railing of the balcony overlooking the room, and he ran down the stairs with that bounding assurance of people who never have to look where they're going. He was wearing a white linen jacket with a dark blue turtleneck shirt, and he looked even more exuberantly handsome than he had that afternoon. Lucy, looking at him, remembered a story she'd heard about a male movie star. A writer friend who'd worked in Holly-wood had told her, "He has a girl before breakfast and another before dinner and another at bedtime, like vitamin capsules. And he thrives on it."

Jason looked thriving. He went over and ran a finger lightly down his wife's cheek. "But she's a good witch, aren't you, darling? She casts nice spells—the kind she put on me."

If Velanie was blushing, it didn't show under the skill-ful, heavy makeup, but she had the air of a woman who was blushing. She said a bit ruefully, "I should have put a curse on you." Then she slapped his hand away.

It was a kind of playfulness that is hard for outsiders to take, especially on an empty stomach. Lucy said, "What a good idea, to convert that end into a dining room," and marched up the three steps determinedly.

The long table was covered with a rosy-red cloth, and the place settings were opulent: gold-bordered service plates, crystal goblets, heavy silver initialed with a curli-cued V. Between the massive silver candlesticks, for a centerpiece, sat a silver wine cooler with one skinny split of champagne standing gravely alone in the crushed ice.

"One split for three people!" Jason exclaimed. "It's too much."

Velanie had seated herself at the head of the table, and motioned Lucy to the place on her right. "I have a business meeting with Wynn after dinner. I can't afford to get drunk."

"Sweetie, even on a whole bottle of champagne, we'll be sober as Baptists." Jason took the seat opposite Lucy and winked at her. "I told the maid to bring in a bottle of Tait-inger's."

"I work, you spend." It was still good-humored grumbling.

"Admit you have more fun for your money now. Ah, here it comes."

Whoever had brought the liquid reinforcements had to go past Lucy. She caught a glimpse of a rosy-red uniform just as a familiar voice said in her ear, "Welcome to Shangri-la-de-da!"

"Mrs. Terrizi!"

Mrs. Terrizi was built low to the ground and always seemed to move slanting forward, at a half-run. The red uniform was tight on her, but the color was marvelously becoming. Like her son the police sergeant, she had eyes as shiny black as ripe olives, and black hair so curly it seemed to crackle.

Lucy said, "How nice to see you. I didn't know you were working here."

"I'm only filling in tonight for my niece."

Velanie said, "Give my husband the champagne —which was *not* ordered by me—and bring in the first course."

"Cock Saint Jack coming right up," Mrs. Terrizi said. "And where I come from, it's the husband who gives the orders."

Jason guffawed. Velanie's scowl deepened, but she sat in brooding silence till the kitchen door closed again. "That one's too fresh."

"She's quite a character," Lucy said. "I've known her for years. She's the mother of a police sergeant I work with on cases."

"You—a detective?" Velanie was amused. "Who would guess?"

"Who indeed?" Jason was staring across at Lucy with an odd expression. "I might have known Velanie would get double value for her money."

Lucy came near saying, Listen, you overage juvenile, I don't spy on two-timing husbands. What she did say, looking at him very steadily, was "You'll be glad to know I only work on murder cases."

Jason instantly switched back to the debonair-charmer role and sparkled at her. "Glad! I'm awed. I'm overcome. We must drink to your sherlocking—or should I say she-locking?" He eased out the cork with an expert non-plop and got up to fill the women's glasses.

Velanie put her hand over the top of her goblet. "None for me."

He bent and kissed the top of her head. "But we can't have a toast if your glass is empty. Come on, darling, just a few swallows. This is a party."

Velanie withdrew her hand. "A teaspoonful."

"She's measured out her life in teaspoons," Jason announced dramatically.

60

Lucy was surprised that an ex-Olympic swimmer knew Eliot's Prufrock. She had a regrettably snobbish notion about what went on in athletes' heads.

Jason picked up a dessert spoon and tilted the bottle with exaggerated care, as if to measure out a spoonful.

"Idiot! You'll spill it," Velanie cried. "Just pour a little into my glass."

He poured more than a little. And he filled his own glass to the brim. "A toast. To the prettiest and most charming of detectives—Mrs. Ramsdale."

Velanie's lower lip stuck out. She made a pretense of taking a sip, but she was obviously sulking.

She won't have anybody else come first, Lucy thought. (It has been said that the faults we recognize most clearly in others are our own.)

Jason had already realized his mistake. "And to Velanie—beauty queen to the world."

Velanie didn't hesitate to drink to herself.

Champagne was Lucy's least favorite wine, but she drank thirstily. "I was seventeen when I had my first champagne. And I complained it tasted like getting water up my nose in swimming."

Jason laughed.

Velanie didn't: "All that money for carbonated water that gives you gas."

The coquilles Saint-Jacques, which were superb, put her in a better humor. She even said thank you to Mrs. Terrizi, who served them in what Lucy considered an ominous silence but may have passed for submissiveness.

"You think I'm right about my chef, eh, Loozy?"

"If you offered me a choice of your chef or your rubies, I'd take the chef."

"The rubies are insured. The chef is not." She was sopping up the sauce with a piece of French bread. "Not fattening, this dish. The best chefs have changed. They use almost no butter or cream any more. A light beef or chicken stock, vegetable oil . . ." She expanded on this anti-cholesterol trend through the main course: rare roast beef (cut too thin), zucchini, and another green vegetable Lucy couldn't place but rather liked.

"Seaweed," Velanie said. "Vitamin K and iodine—very healthy. Celia and I learned about it in Japan, their kombu. For years, Celia always traveled with me. Poor little one, her nose is out of joint now. She is jealous of Jason. You will see—she hardly speaks to him."

Lucy looked mischievously at Jason, who grimaced, and then, as Velanie switched her attention back to the mopping-up-sauce operation, he raised his hands palms up in a gesture of supplication to his tormentor: *Have pity on me.*

"I'm glad I don't have Celia in the pool," he said. "She's so heavy-minded she'd sink like cement."

"She takes work seriously. Which is something you can't understand. You take nothing seriously."

"Oh, I do, I do. I took *you* seriously, darling, when you promised me a Maserati."

"There was a good-looking red Mercedes in the parking lot this afternoon," Lucy purred. "Did you happen to notice it?"

This time, Jason looked definitely uneasy.

Velanie grunted. "Too common—Mercedes. All over the place now. I used to have a Mercedes three hundred, but my husband the prince preferred a Maserati."

"So do I." Jason refilled his glass.

"We'll see."

"You've been saying that for six months."

His wife ignored this. "Loozy, I will have our best operator give you the hot honey mask, tomorrow. There is nothing else like it in the world. You want massage, too?"

Lucy said she'd have the works. "But make all my appointments in the afternoon. I want to sketch in the mornings."

"You see," Velanie said to her husband, "Loozy puts work first. Like Celia."

Lucy didn't fancy being classed with Celia, and she felt a bit guilty about having baited Jason. "When do you have a class at the pool?" He said underwater exercise was at eleven-thirty. "I'd like to sketch you and some of your whales."

"Make them minnows." Velanie sounded good-humored again. "Him you can sketch as is. In swim trunks, he's not too bad."

Jason jumped up and flung out his arms. "Attention, ladies! To stretch the pectoral muscles—these few simple strokes under water." His arms wove in and out while his chest swelled like a tire being pumped. Next he clasped his hands in front of his stomach. "Pit your arm muscles against each other—hard, harder—to lift and youthify your breasts. What does a man look at first?" Leer. "Exactly."

Lucy and Velanie were laughing. Mrs. Terrizi, who had come in to remove the plates, put an end to the performance. "It's nine o'clock," she said loudly. "If you want anything else, you'll take it now or get it yourself. My niece told me dinner's at six in this place and I'd be out of here by eight. Some story."

Velanie gestured imperiously. "Mrs. Whatever-your-name-is, let me see your skin close to."

Mrs. Terrizi was so surprised she obeyed.

"Closer." Velanie grabbed one of Mrs. Terrizi's sturdy wrists and yanked, while with the other hand she lifted a

63

heavy candlestick and brought the candle flame up like a torch.

Mrs. Terrizi let out a screech. "If you think you're gonna burn me—"

"Shush. Your pores are too big. I'll give you the right cream tomorrow. You're too young and attractive to let yourself go."

Mrs. Terrizi was digesting this in dazed silence when the phone rang. As if it awakened her from a spell, she shot off, skidded down the three steps, and raced the length of the room to answer it. "Madame Velanie's residence . . . It's for you." She motioned vigorously to Jason.

"That's the salesman for the underwater equipment. He said he'd go over a price list and give me figures. I'd better take the call in my room." He loped up the stairs, and as soon as they heard a door shut, Velanie said, "I must get the papers from my room for Arnold to go over tonight." She was halfway up the stairs, moving with surprising speed and lightness, when she remembered something. "Loozy, you have dessert."

"Just coffee," Lucy called to Mrs. Terrizi, who was holding on to the receiver waiting to hang up. At least, that was what Mrs. Terrizi was doing until Velanie disappeared. Then she cuddled the receiver against her ear and listened avidly.

When she finally eased the receiver onto the hook, she came back and told Lucy in what was, for Mrs. Terrizi, a low voice, "That was no underwater salesman. It was a dame and she called him Jason. And Madame got on the extension in her room—I heard the click. The dame wants him to meet her in the Oaks taproom because she's bored." Mrs. Terrizi's black eyes sparkled. "Wait'll Madame gets hold of him now. *He* won't be bored."

64

Lucy made a face. "I'm ducking out before the main bout."

"Tell you what, I'll bring you over a pot of coffee. Where'd they put you?"

Ten minutes later, Mrs. Terrizi kicked the terrace door in lieu of knocking. She was carrying a pot of coffee in one hand, a bowl of fresh fruit in the other, and the latest news between her teeth. "Madame was pounding on his door, and he kept yelling, 'I'm in the bathroom!' So Madame goes off to some meeting carrying a briefcase with a funny bulge—like a gun. I was telling Nicky somebody's gonna be mopping up blood around here. He says, 'Mama, don't you go drumming up business for the inspector and me.' And I tell him, 'I don't hafta—the war drums are already rolling.' Is that why they sent you out here? To keep your ear to the wall?"

Lucy said crossly nobody had sent her. "I'm here to do some sketches."

"Good excuse. I gotta go now. See you tomorrow."

Lucy ate a pear, finished her coffee, and investigated the bedside reading on the under shelf of the night table. There were several books: *Eat Away Your Own Fat . . . From I Chin to Gung Ho . . . Follow Your Star and Shine.* Lucy, a renegade Virgo who went along with Mark Antony and Shakespeare on the astrology bit, was relieved to find a paperback mystery just underneath, probably left by some light-minded former occupant. She upended the two implacably hard bed pillows, kicked off her pumps, and settled down on the bed to read about a woman psychiatrist, an amateur detective *manqué*, who thought any man who wanted to marry her was a possessive chauvinist pig. Soon after eleven, Lucy threw the book across the room with a final muttered "Christ!" and was about to undress when she heard a tap on her terrace door.

65

A man's voice called softly, "Are you decent? May I come in? I have to see you. It's important."

Lucy pulled back the curtain, saw Jason through the glass, and opened the door just a crack. "No, you may not come in. I refuse to get involved in your silly games."

"Look, it's not a game. I'm in trouble."

He did look pale; either desperation or bad lighting gave him a washed-out pallor that was quite becoming.

"I'll come out on the terrace for exactly two minutes."

"Not out here." His whisper was fiercely urgent. "Somebody would see us."

"Who cares?"

Jason said virtuously, "I'm only thinking of your reputation."

It was so ridiculous, and so impudent, Lucy couldn't help laughing. "Oh, all right. Come in for a minute."

Once inside, Jason helped himself instantly to a bunch of hothouse grapes and sprawled out in a ruffled boudoir chair. "You're an angel for not giving me away at dinner. I know you saw me behind the hedge after I left Celia. She didn't even hear the car. That girl is insane—acting like a lovesick dairymaid."

"You're a great one to talk. Who made her lovesick in the first place?"

"If I'd known what I was getting into! She was so cool and contained—she didn't even *like* me. So naturally I wanted to see if she was really as cold as she seemed." He spat a grape seed into his hand and groaned. "Like unleashing a bitch in heat. She's insatiable."

"A virgin kept on ice too long thaws out too fast." Lucy heard what she'd said and thought it had the authentic ring of an old Chinese proverb.

"*Now* you tell me! She's already flooding over. Talks

about how she loves me and 'we mustn't do anything to hurt Velanie' but 'someday we'll be together for always.' Hurt Velanie! can you imagine what she'd do to us if she learned? You heard her at dinner—'That dear, devoted child Celia.' What can I do to get that girl off my neck?"

"Tell her it's over."

"You don't know her. If she congealed again, she'd bury me like an avalanche. She'd go to Velanie and say I'd been trying to lay her and it was her loyal duty to show me up as a faithless bastard."

"Well, you are. And Velanie must already know it."

"Oh, she knows I play around a bit. But that's different. She blows her top and I eat crow and we kiss and make up. You know, I'm really fond of the old girl."

"You're pushing your luck. That alibi about the salesman for underwater equipment—pretty feeble."

"I was caught off guard. How should I know that woman would call me here? I only met her this afternoon in a bar."

"And you told her you loved her for her red Mercedes."

"You're too sharp. You really had me squirming at dinner. And the hell of it is, I think Velanie listened in on the call."

"She did. I hear you took shelter afterward in the bathroom."

Jason pulled out of his sprawling position in a hurry. "How did you know?"

"Omniscience. You're lucky Velanie had to go off to that meeting."

"Luckier than you know. Right now she and that scruffy ex-husband are going over sweet fat figures—business profits—and that always mellows her. By the time she gets back, I can handle her."

He didn't actually paw the ground, but he gave that impression. Prize bull, Lucy thought. You cost more than you're worth.

"But if Velanie learns about Celia—" He was no longer playing the prize bull; he was hunched as if for a blow. "She'd kick us out and see that nobody else hired us. Or she might kill us both."

Lucy looked at him sharply. She had a feeling this was what he'd been working up to all along—even why he'd come in the first place.

"So you can see why I count on you to keep mum. You will, won't you?"

"Spare me the boyish-appeal act."

Jason said in a hurt tone, "I thought you were simpatico."

"You thought I'd be easily gulled."

"That was stupid of me," he said cheerfully. "But if you won't keep quiet about Celia for my sake, then do it for Velanie's. She's too—"

The phone tinkled. "If that's Velanie, you haven't seen me."

Lucy was already listening to the agitated voice at the other end: "Mrs. Ramsdale, this is the switchboard operator. We're not allowed to put through calls to the guests after nine-thirty P.M. But this man says it's urgent police business. He says he's Inspector McDougal. Do you know anybody by that name?"

"Yes, I know Inspector McDougal very well. Put him on."

Jason was making frantic gestures, finger to lips: *Don't blab.*

Lucy gestured: *Out.* When he didn't budge, she murmured, "Get going, you underwater Don Juan."

Inspector McDougal said, "I can't hear you. Something about under water."

I said, "Underwater Don Juan. But I wasn't talking to you. I was talking to a man in my room."

"In your room?" McDougal's voice went up several decibels. "But you aren't even allowed to get phone calls this late. Who is he?"

Lucy was enjoying herself. "Oh, he's just somebody else's husband. Hang on till I push him out the door."

As she got up, Jason said "Tattletale," and ducked out.

Lucy came back to the phone, which was crackling: ". . . thought that place was for women only."

"Jason works here. Tell me, what's the urgent business?"

The inspector said, "I had to tell the operator that. She wouldn't put my call through. I wanted to make sure you were all right. Has—er—anybody bothered you?"

"No, why should they?"

"I thought you might be—well—avoiding somebody by staying at the spa."

"What a silly idea."

McDougal said stiffly it was even sillier to go to a beauty spa for no reason. "I didn't think you were such a featherhead."

"I happen to be here on assignment, to do some sketches." Having had to explain this three times in one evening, Lucy was ready to erupt. "And why the hell should you track me down, anyway?"

"I was worried about you. I couldn't reach you at home."

This was so un-McDougalish, and so disarming, Lucy melted. "I should have called you in New York and told you I'd be gone for a while. How did you know where to find me? Oh, Mrs. Terrizi."

"She gave Nicky some big story about the people who run the place. She said somebody's going to be mopping up blood."

"That was just wishful thinking."

But by the time Lucy put out her bedside light, she was feeling less flip. When Jason had said, "Velanie would kill us both," it had seemed ridiculously melodramatic. But consciously or not, had he really meant "We'll have to shut her up first"?

A phrase she hadn't thought of for over fifty years surfaced suddenly. When she'd been very young, her father had often told her a bedtime story about a child who ran away and went into a forbidden woods: "And the farther she went, the deeper, the darker." The repeated phrase "the deeper, the darker," for some perverse reason unknown to child psychologists, had always sent the small Lucy to sleep. Probably because her father had repeated it more and more slowly, till his listener was bored into oblivion. And she couldn't remember that she'd ever had nightmares about it. But now the phrase didn't lull her; it made her feel prickly.

To soothe herself, she went back to thinking about McDougal's phone call. He had actually admitted he'd worried about her. As if she couldn't look after herself. But she was glad she didn't look like a woman who can always look after herself.

5

THE YOUNG MAID who brought Lucy's breakfast tray at seven was surprised to find the room empty. She was used to rousing the ladies with anything from a cheery but penetrating "Good morning" to a genteel shake of a snoring form burrowed in rose-strewn blankets. The door of the adjoining bathroom was wide open, but just to make sure, the maid listened to find out if the shower was running. It wasn't. She next checked the closet, not because she expected to find a body, but to see if the lady's exercise suit was still hanging there. It was. She had heard of one or two hardy types who went out jogging even before breakfast, but she was fairly new at this job—she had been a chambermaid at the Oaks Inn—and she'd never met one of the rise-at-dawn dynamos herself. She had left the tray on the bed; now she rechecked the hand-lettered card propped against the thermos jug of coffee: "Mrs. Ramsdale—Jade Empress—Room 5."

"Mrs. Ramsdale," she called, bending down as if she expected Mrs. Ramsdale to crawl from under the bed. This had happened to her once at the Oaks—and had left an indelible impression.

71

"Out here."

The heavy curtains on the rear wall were only partly open. The maid yanked cords and peered out. Lucy was sitting at the drafting table on the terrace, sketching. She wore a long white nylon lace robe, and over it a violet-blue smock the color of her eyes. "Good morning. Did you bring my breakfast?"

The maid said in a surprised tone, "Gee, you look pretty." She had been trained, like all the staff, to give the so-called guests praise and encouragement, but this outburst was quite spontaneous.

Lucy was one of those women who wake up bright-eyed and delectable even without makeup. And she was used to accepting compliments naturally, as her due. She smiled at the young maid and cleared a space in front of her, on the table. "What a nice way to start the day. I'll eat out here."

Her tone changed sharply when she looked at the breakfast tray. A round, flat, greenish-mud-colored object, two inches in diameter, sat on a plate, the only edible solid in sight. "What the hell's this?"

"Tofu, madam. A combination of soybean curd and dried kelp. It has as much protein as one egg, without the calories." She recited this as she'd been taught, then said doubtfully, "It don't look very tasty, does it? There's toast wrapped in the napkin."

The "toast" was one wafer-thin slice of whole-wheat bread, unbuttered.

"And there's juice in that glass."

The "juice," a pale tan liquid in a glass not much bigger than a jigger, nestled in a bowl of ice, looking even lonelier than Velanie's split of champagne the night before.

Lucy's appetite was almost invariably good, but in the

morning it was rapacious. She rolled her eyes upward appealingly. "I'm not on a diet. I'm here to work, just like you, and we working girls have to stoke up. Would it get you into trouble if you sneaked me in a big glass of orange juice, two scrambled eggs soft, and three or four slices of bacon, and sugar for my coffee?"

The young maid had been hooked from "here to work, just like you." She was back in less than fifteen minutes with the order, plus, as she pointed out, "Two pats of real butter."

Lucy thanked her prettily and tackled her breakfast, but the girl didn't want to leave. "Could I see the picture you're painting?"

Years before, a teacher at the Art Students' League had warned his class, Lucy among them, "Never show an unfinished work to fools or children." But this was no time to cavil, not with a mouthful of contraband scrambled eggs. Lucy held up her sketch pad for better viewing.

"Gee, it's real cute."

The hawthorn tree was considerably better than that. Lucy had started work on it zestfully at 6:30 A.M. She had gone to sleep thinking about the inspector and had wakened at six in a splendid humor. McDougal's disapproval of her being there had sharpened her determination to do a bang-up job, and made her totally concentrated on work. She'd just begun sketching in figures in the foreground, on the tennis court, but for some reason they felt all wrong, and she welcomed the interruption for breakfast.

The lanky young maid was still looking over Lucy's shoulder. "Hardly any of the ladies play tennis." Lucy stiffened with annoyance and willed the kibitzer to go away. "Mostly they jog."

Jog! That was it. Put three or four small figures in front

73

of the tree, maybe in a curve—much fresher and more all of a piece. Lucy dropped a piece of bacon she'd been eating with her fingers and grabbed a drawing pencil. "You're so right. Bring me that exercise suit from the closet."

The maid, charmed to be part of the creative process, rushed to produce the sweat suit, a rather washed-out red cotton knit.

Lucy regarded the baggy thing with distaste. "I'll have to wait till I see it on somebody."

"You want I should try it on for you?"

The girl was tall—at least five feet nine—and built like a broomstick.

Lucy said she'd already taken up too much of the maid's time. "I'll walk around the place later till I spot what I want."

"Would you call the kitchen when you're through, so I can come sneak the tray away myself? Ask for Mavis. There's a card by the phone that gives all the extensions."

"You've been wonderful, Mavis. May I do a sketch of you before I leave? I'd like to give it to you as a little thank-you."

Mavis left in a state bordering on ecstasy.

The scrambled eggs were still warm; the bacon was cool but crisp. Lucy was on her second cup of coffee when she saw a lone jogger in the distance, elbows churning, dogged as the runner to García, if less speedy.

Lucy sketched swiftly. To give the figure more style, she tied the baggy pants at the ankle like harem trousers, tapered the waist, and added a striped turban. By the time she'd added three more figures, spaced out, after obliterating the tennis court, she was so pleased with the result that she opened her box of watercolor paints, hauled out the muffin tin she used for mixing colors, and set to.

"It's absolutely enchanting," Adele Vining was saying, an hour later. She was wearing a pale pink blazer and perfectly cut white pants, and she looked and seemed more relaxed than she had the day before. "Lewis was much better by the time I got there. He sent his love to you. Right now he can't have any visitors, but he hopes to see you before we leave for Zurich. Did Velanie tell you?"

Lucy said Celia Grant had. "She said you'd tell me how generous Velanie is." Lucy's voice was dryly skeptical.

"It's true—in spurts. And thank God I was one of her spurts. She'd heard about the doctor in Zurich, and last week she gave me a check for ten thousand—just like that."

"At what interest?"

"It's a gift. Not a string attached. So even when I get furious at her sometimes, I just count to ten thousand and forgive her. She's really fantastic, you know. Still works with her chemists in the lab, tries out all the new products on herself, and does everything from Yoga exercises to swinging dumbbells—of all the ludicrous extremes. She must have a dozen sets of dumbbells scattered around—in her offices and houses."

"I'm surprised she doesn't wear gym bloomers and a middy blouse."

"Don't underestimate her. She's astonishingly ahead on her products. She was the first woman in the cosmetics field to bring out a line for men. I suspect she dreamed up this spa as a tax loss—prestige, if no profit. Of course, she spent at least a million setting it up. Then she'll stew about the cost of paper clips."

Lucy described the split of champagne, and Jason's ordering reinforcements.

"He's the only one who could get away with it. Velanie

75

humors him, up to a point." Adele was sitting in the chair Jason had sat in the night before, and Lucy came near telling her about his nocturnal call, but she wasn't sure how much Adele knew, and felt reluctant to squeal.

"I can't understand why Velanie married him instead of just keeping him as a pet."

"She was a peasant, and peasants are very conventional. And realistic. She knows Jason's a beautiful hunk of male and she can't keep him from having other women. The one-night stands—or lays—aren't that important. I doubt if she's ever cared much about sex herself. But if Jason deceives her in any serious way, and she finds out, God help him."

Adele knows about Celia but she wants to avoid an explosion, Lucy thought. Aloud, she said, "I want to do some sketches in his class at eleven-thirty, at the pool, and in the meantime I'll take a look at the exercise rooms."

Adele said they were all in the basement. "I'll take you down and introduce you to Miss Tringle, the program director."

She picked up the sketch Lucy had finished, handling it tenderly by one corner. "Let's take this along to Velanie first. Her office is just at the other end of the corridor."

Lucy said she'd rather wait till she'd done several more.

"But this is such a delicious foretaste." Adele sounded almost pleading. "If she's in a foul mood, this would cheer her up."

And keep her from yelling at you? "All right. Give me five minutes to change." Lucy picked up the exercise suit lying on the bed. "God, do I have to wear this thing? Yes, I'd better. If I look as awful as the other women, they'll be more relaxed with me."

When she came out of the bathroom dressed, or at least

76

covered, Adele burst out laughing. "It fits you like a blanket."

The rest of the costume consisted of terry-cloth scuffs, but they were so floppy Lucy changed to her own sneakers. When she stowed her gear back in her carryall and picked it up, she felt like herself again.

In the corridor, Adele turned left and led her past two closed doors inscribed with elaborate gold lettering: YELLOW DIAMOND and MAHARAJAH'S RUBY.

"They ran out of jewels for the upstairs bedrooms. Amethyst and opal sounded too cheap. So they named the others after Velanie's lipsticks. Be glad you aren't in Pink Witch or Red Devil."

The last door in that wing, just beyond Maharajah's Ruby, was labeled, incongruously, DIRECTRESS, MISS GRANT.

"I know what I'd name that one," Adele muttered. "Pink Bitch. But I'll admit Celia's fiendishly efficient. She's the one who really runs this place. Velanie's in New York or Europe half the time, but we're lucky she's here now. I can hardly wait to have her see your work."

They had gone past the door to the main hall, past a small elevator, and were halfway to the end of the corridor when Velanie's voice roared out: "She never had a brother or stepbrother, you idiot. You were drunk."

"Whatever that's about," Adele said, "she's on a rampage. I'll have to give her time to cool down."

Lucy could guess what it was about: Celia Grant's mythical sibling, or half-sibling. Arnold Wynn must have waked up cold sober, figured things out, and decided, out of mischief or altruism, to alert his ex-wife. Lucy hoped he wouldn't succeed.

"We'll leave the sketch in my office." Adele opened the door marked PUBLICITY. "Come on in a second."

The office was about one-quarter the size of the old office Lucy remembered Adele in, at the magazine. But it had the same pale yellow walls and a beautifully simple blond wood desk and three chairs that looked like Coggeshall designs. Above the desk was a small painting, the head of a man, that was oddly like a Rouault, the gaunt elongated face and burned-out eye sockets.

"A painter friend of ours did it of Lewis last spring."

It was so unlike the Lewis Vining she'd known that Lucy's throat tightened and all she could manage was something about "strong," which can mean strong as in powerful, or strong as in medicine.

Adele seemed not to notice. She was putting Lucy's sketch on her desk, next to a small tape recorder. "I'll have Miss Simms, the secretary, take it in. She has the office next door and presumably Velanie and I share her, but Velanie works the poor woman ten hours a day. So I dictate letters and releases on tape—and half the time I type them myself. But I'm thankful for Simms anyway, because she takes the brunt of the tantrums. And when Velanie's calmed down, I'll go bask in your reflected glory."

Lucy, who was used to basking in her own glory, was pointedly silent. Adele misunderstood. "You needn't worry about my sending Simms into battle. She's had over twenty years of being a punching bag. It must gratify her deepest masochistic instincts. No, that's not fair. She's more like a mattress you can bounce on. When Lewis and I were first lovers, we went to a funny little hotel on Second Avenue and signed in as Mr. and Mrs.—I forget who. And the bed broke down—the slats or something—so we dragged the mattress onto the floor and went right on with what we were doing. Seeing you takes me back to those lovely lost days. Don't let me cry or I'll smear my Velanie waterproof mascara."

Lucy supplied the right astringent tone. "If I don't get back to work and earn my keep, we'll both be in trouble."

The small self-service elevator that took them down one flight was so ornately rose and gold that Lucy said she felt like a bird in a gilded cage. But as soon as they stepped out onto the bare concrete floor of the basement, the atmosphere was strongly gymnasium. Not that the place smelled of anything so indelicate as sweat—it was more the aura of strenuous purpose.

A woman who looked as if she were made of loosely packed beanbags was being weighed on the scales near the elevator, by an instructor in rosy-red shorts and halter who was not loosely packed. "Oh, good girl, Mrs. Volter. Another pound and five-eighths off." A second instructor cracked her metal tape measure like a whip. "Now let's see about those hips, Mrs. Volter. . . . *Three inches* lost since last week! You deserve a gold medal." Mrs. Volter's eyes glistened with tears of—presumably—joy.

As Adele and Lucy started down the corridor, a voice came booming from behind a closed door. "The stones are red hot and the water is boiling. I'm ready to work on you, Mrs. Farleigh."

Another voice, thinner and quavering: "Are you going to beat me with birch branches?"

"My God," Lucy said. "Do they pay fifteen hundred a week to be boiled and beaten?"

"That's the sauna." Adele was frowning. "I must say the attendant isn't too tactful."

As if to confirm this remark, the booming voice said, "In Sweden, we beat with the branches. Not here—American ladies are too nervous."

"I'm damned if I'll sketch *that*," Lucy said.

They passed several more young attendants or instructors heading toward the elevator—all young with good figures, and all bearing a curious bodily resemblance to each other, as if they'd been made from interchangeable parts that might even be grafted onto a client.

One of the girls broke loose to hail Adele. "Oh, Mrs. Vining, will you go to Miss Grant's office right away? She has an urgent message for you."

Adele grabbed Lucy's arm so tightly it hurt. "If the nursing home called about Lewis . . . I'm sorry—I'll have to leave you. Miss Baskie, this is Mrs. Ramsdale. She's doing an important assignment for Madame Velanie and she's to go wherever she likes."

Lucy said quietly, "Adele, would you like me to come with you?"

Adele shook her head and tried to smile. "It's probably nothing. Some beauty editor doing a story—they always think everything's urgent."

At the elevator, she turned to wave, in a gallant attempt at cheerfulness.

Miss Baskie said, "Would you like me to conduct you around, Mrs. Ramsdale?"

Lucy loathed the idea of being conducted; she said she'd rather roam around by herself.

Miss Baskie had sniffed the musky scent of publicity, and was reluctant to let her go. "If you don't have any special class in mind, I'm giving a session in positive vibrations at nine-thirty."

To get rid of the girl, Lucy said, "Perhaps another day."

Miss Baskie hung on. "The thing is, we try to improve not only the clients' looks, but their *outlook on life*. And you'd be amazed at the difference in just a short time. One client was so changed—mentally and physically—she wrote us such a charming letter afterward saying that when she got home, even her dog didn't know her. He tried to bite her."

80

"How about her husband? Did he try to bite her?"

"She was a widow at the time," Miss Baskie said. "She has since been remarried, to a very wealthy man."

"Did he know her Before, or only After?"

Miss Baskie backed away on that one. Lucy went down the corridor, past the door marked MASSAGE, stopped dead at WHIRLPOOL, and opened that door cautiously. Nothing but three empty bathtubs in three open cubicles. Gone down for the third time, evidently.

The door just beyond Whirlpool was wide open, to display an arresting tableau: four women in exercise suits were hanging upside down on objects that looked like ironing boards. These seemed to thrust into the air at a forty-five-degree angle without any means of support, except perhaps supernatural. This eerie effect was intensified when Lucy went in to take a closer look: all the women had their eyes closed and seemed not to be breathing. Their hands were folded across their chests in a pose once favored by undertakers.

A voice from nowhere, like a genteel lady·sergeant's, said suddenly, "And *thirteen!* Breathe out."

A whoosh of exhalations stirred the air. One of the upside-downers opened her eyes, pulled up her pudgy chin a trifle, and said "Hi."

It was nice to know the victims could still talk. Or at least one of them could. She had a full, round face and looked rather like an outsize baby in a fright wig: her streaked blond hair was as spiky as a haystack.

The stomach of another hanger-on, a younger woman, stuck out like a watermelon. Lucy hoped to God the woman wasn't pregnant: the child might turn out oddly—like a bat or something.

This woman said very nicely to Lucy, "Good morning. You must have just come. Miss Tringle had an urgent call to go to Madame Velanie's . . ." It seemed to be a day for urgent calls. ". . . so she put on a tape. That's Miss Tringle's voice on the recording. Have you tried this Yoga slant?" She had the finishing-school accent on "slant," one of those people who say "frightful awss" for "ass." "So much easier than the bit of standing on one's head."

Lucy said she hadn't tried either stance. Her artist's eye was already at work, blocking in the scene, respacing the boards, reminding herself to minimize the stomach bulge. With a twinge of regret she thought, George Grosz would have made the bulge even bigger. None of the other women had so outstanding a problem, at least judging them upside down. The face on the board farthest from her looked fuzzily familiar; she thought it must be somebody from Wingate she'd seen around town.

The voice on the tape deck blared, in a ladylike way: "Are those thighs communing with the boards? Tight— tight—tighter."

The women adjusted their hips and went rigid.

The voice in the box went on: "Let the bloodstream have a clear, smooth path to your brain. Scientific tests have shown that the brain works *sixteen percent better* when your feet are above your head. Remember, you are fighting gravity—the enemy that pulls you down and makes those horrid sags we have to get rid of. The early cave-persons crawled around on all fours and were as healthy and chock-full of energy as animals. Then we learned to stand on two feet and that's where the trouble began. Why? Because nature did *not* intend us to be vertical—we were meant to be horizontal."

The woman who looked familiar was yawning. The others were reverently solemn as the voice finished its sermon. At the risk of sounding sacrilegious, Lucy said briskly, "Do you mind if I sketch you? Velanie asked me to do some sketches they'll use in *Vogue* and other magazines."

Moon-face made a gurgling sound of pleasure, but the others were uneasily silent till Lucy said, "Of course, I wouldn't make your faces recognizable. But I'd love to catch you just as you are."

This time, stomach-bulge said it sounded like a fun thing; a woman with a blue rinse and crêpey throat agreed, and moon-face gurgled again. Lucy had just pulled her sketch pad out of the carryall, and was reaching into one of the outside compartments for a drawing pencil, when the woman on the board farthest from her said sharply, "Leave me out. Velanie promised me I'd have complete privacy here and not be pestered by reporters or photographers. And that goes for small-town artists, too."

Lucy knew that voice, which reminded her of a brook babbling over gravel. No wonder the woman looked familiar: she was Marta Galt, a well-known interviewer on a morning television show.

Lucy went over and looked down at the celebrated face. "I wouldn't have known you," she cooed. "You look so much older off camera—and without all that clever makeup they put on you in the studio. The makeup man must be a genius."

Marta Galt used an imperative verb that would have had her bleeped off the air in two seconds.

Finishing-school-accent said quickly to Lucy, "I've been admiring that marvelous bag of yours." She had that well-bred instinct to throw trivia into the cannon's mouth, either to deflect the line of fire or to muffle the noise. "Where *did* you find it?"

"It was a present." Lucy, still seething, added deliber-

83

ately, "From a police inspector I know. I helped him solve several murders in Wingate, and this carryall was a little thank-you."

"Rams—rams—ramsgate," Marta Galt muttered. "Now I know who you are. We talked one time about getting you and Inspector Whosis on our show."

"It's Ramsdale—not Ramsgate. And neither Inspector McDougal nor I would consider being on your show." (This was stretching the truth to the point of no return where Lucy was concerned. She adored an audience— even an audience of six or eight million breakfast-eating viewers.) "You're too rude and nosy."

Unexpectedly, Marta Galt laughed. "It gets results. Look, I'm sorry I gave you the flake-off. Are you really here to sketch, or did Velanie hire you to do some investigating on the side?"

Lucy said coolly, "I'm an artist. I am not a private eye."

"But you have a way of being around when somebody gets killed. And believe me, Ramsdale, you've come to the right place. I knew Velanie's Jason all too well in New York before—"

"Draw in your stomachs!" the absent Miss Tringle commanded. "In and *up*. In and *up*. In and *up*. Now hold till the count of fourteen. This is the cure for what we call jelly belly. If you do it every—"

"Turn that thing off," Marta Galt told moon-face. "Mrs. Ramsdale can't work with that yak going on."

Lucy decided she rather liked the woman after all.

Moon-face reached down near her head, pressed a button, and the board lowered itself sedately. Lucy, who had gone to the back of the room to fetch a small chair, saw the mechanism at work and thought, Like a hospital bed gone mad. Moon-face rolled off, got up wheezing, and padded over to the small tape deck in the corner, where she had second thoughts. "Do you really think I should? Miss Tringle won't like it."

Miss Tringle's disembodied voice solved the problem. "And now for our second ten minutes in Yoga slant," it said, "we will have total quiet for Zen meditation. As Adam Smith says in his *Powers of the Mind*, Zen meditation is like having a mini-vacation. Think of it, ladies— you may have a mini-vacation twice each day. Now put your thoughts on this beautiful koan: 'I stand on the bank of a river. The bank flows but the river stands still.' Contemplate the inner meaning. Now, quiet."

Lucy had already set up her chair at the front of the room, got out her 20″ x 24″ drawing pad, and was sketching with a sure hand. Moon-face hurried to remount her board and get back in the picture. She, stomach-bulge, and blue-rinse closed their eyes and contemplated the flowing bank, perhaps its liquid assets. Marta Galt closed one eye in an unmistakable wink, and was quiet, too.

By the time Miss Tringle's voice said "End of vacation. Now back on your feet," Lucy had roughed in all four figures. Before the women could assume the vertical position and crowd around to take a look, she stuck her pad in her carryall. "Thanks so much. I'll go back to my room to work on it while the details are fresh in my mind."

Moon-face asked, "When can we see it?"

"In a day or two."

Stomach-bulge wanted to know if Mrs. Rahmsdale was sketching in other "clawsses."

Lucy said the only one she'd decided on was underwater exercise at eleven-thirty. Three of the women chorused their pleasure. "Then we'll see you at the pool."

Marta Galt was more persistent and more agile, so that

she was on her feet almost instantly to follow Lucy into the corridor. Right side up, she was an attractive, if square-jawed, brunette of around forty.

"Remember, if you come up with a body, I want an exclusive for my show."

"I'm not going to kill somebody just to get on your show."

"Why not? Other people have—more or less. But all you have to do is discover a corpse."

"God forbid."

Lucy, back on her terrace, worked contentedly. To get more contrast to the exercise suits of the upside-down figures, she had made each Yoga-slant board a different color instead of their oatmeal beige: green, yellow, turquoise, and, for Marta Galt, shiny black. The television star's dark brown hair didn't show up against the black, so Lucy gave her a drastic bleach. And moon-face, hanging on the green board, got a reddish tint and a sleek new hairdo. Even in art school, Lucy had had a knack of catching an instant likeness. Now it was hard for her to temper that talent enough to make the women unrecognizable, as she'd promised. She didn't altogether succeed, probably because she didn't want to. But she told herself the faces were so small it didn't really matter. And she was scrupulous about minimizing defects like the stomach bulge, not so much to please Adele and Velanie as to avoid being cruel.

The bright colored boards, and even the shiny black, gave a carnival gaiety to the sketch. Add a bouquet in the upper right-hand corner? As if it had been thrown to a performer? Floating free à la Chagall. Yes. Ought to be roses—Velanie's trademark. To hell with roses. Needed lots of color. When she remembered finally to look at her watch, it was already three minutes after eleven-thirty. Damn. She was so involved with the bouquet that having to leave was like a physical wrenching away. She yanked off her smock, pulled the top sheet—the almost finished sketch—off her pad, and weighted it by the corners on the table with her paint box and several brushes. Then she stuck the pad back in her carryall and was ready to take off. If she went around the back way, to the other side of the house, that ought to be the quickest. She spotted the bubble-dome top as soon as she rounded the corner but there was no back entrance to the pool. Walking more slowly down the forty or fifty feet to the other end, she could see Jason through the glass wall, standing on the edge of the pool, demonstrating the exercises he'd hammed at dinner: hands locked, pushing against each other "to lift and youthify the breasts." He was in red swimming trunks, the black hair gleaming wetly on his bare chest, and she was glad to see there wasn't enough hair to look furry. She had never liked furry-chested men.

She stopped to admire him impersonally as a model-to-be: good long legs, flat stomach, neck beautifully joined to the torso. The heads of his half-dozen listeners, in white swim caps, were just visible above the surface of the pool. Do them as rubber-ball faces floating on turquoise water? Too cutesy-artsy. Pose several of the women sitting on the edge of the pool, dangling their legs over? No, lying on their backs with their feet flailing the air. The image of Jason with three females on their backs at once made her laugh out loud.

She had put her heavy carryall down on the grass. When she bent to pick it up, ready to move on and find the entrance, she glanced in once more and was startled to see Celia Grant clutching Jason's arm, talking to him.

Celia was wearing a white pleated skirt as brief as a tennis dress, and the feeling of urgency she gave off seemed incongruous with her costume. Jason was scowling and shaking his head, but as Lucy watched, he seemed to give in. He raised one hand in a gesture of *Attention, ladies.* Then he spoke for perhaps a half-minute, before he turned and followed Celia into what looked like a side passageway, probably connecting to the house.

Lucy considered going in just to show herself to the women. See, I came as I said I would. And she was curious to know what kind of emergency would yank Jason away from his class. Another urgent call to go to Velanie? But then she saw Miss Baskie come in through the same passageway, and it looked as if she were taking over the class. So it couldn't be much of an emergency. Lucy hadn't been drawn to Miss Baskie on their first meeting, and she was stubbornly, even meanly, determined not to feature her in any sketch. She decided to cover the class another day when Jason was back in charge. And she welcomed the chance to finish her Yoga-slant sketch.

She was just touching up the last flower of the bouquet, a brilliant red zinnia, when the phone rang. In her total absorption, the sound startled her enough so that her hand holding the brush jerked and left a messy smear on the white background. She was so exasperated she slammed the brush down on the table and went inside to pick up the phone by the bed. "Yes."

"The sketch is very good." The "good" was Velanie's "goot." Lucy started to say something, but Velanie was still talking, or at least making quacking sounds that were impossible to understand. Then her voice came through more clearly again. "I want to see you in my office right now." Before Lucy could say anything, the receiver on the other end was banged down.

Of all the arrogance . . . Maybe everybody else around here jumps when they're summoned, but not me. If the sketch is that good, she can come and tell me so. While Lucy stood beside the phone still fuming, there was a knock at the door and Adele Vining stuck her head in. "Did she call you? She's crazy about your sketch. She wants to see you right away."

"Let her wait. The woman has no manners. Come on out and see my new sketch. It's even better than the first one."

Adele followed Lucy onto the terrace, but she barely glanced at the sketch. "Yes, charming. We haven't time now. Lucy, she didn't mean to be rude—not to you. All she wants is to tell you herself how delighted she is. She even wants to pay you a fee, because she's going to have new exercise suits and turbans made from your design."

Now that Lucy was mollified, she could take in that Adele looked tense and haggard again. "Was the message about Lewis?"

Adele said in a choked voice, "What message? What do you mean?"

Poor Adele. Lucy said gently, "The message left for you this morning. That girl in the basement told you."

"Oh, that." Adele laughed rather hysterically. "*Harper's Bazaar* wanting to check on a caption before they went to press. That's an emergency!"

Lucy went over to the dressing table to put on fresh lipstick and comb her hair, but Adele said, "Don't bother. We'll only have to stay with Velanie a few minutes. Then you can come back here before we go to lunch in the main dining room. Or we'll have something sent to your room."

Going down the corridor, past Yellow Diamond, Maharajah's Ruby, and Celia Grant's office, Adele moved at such a fast clip Lucy felt both annoyance and compassion, thinking, She's afraid to keep Velanie waiting one extra minute.

But at the office door, MADAME VELANIE—PRIVATE, Adele hesitated. "Maybe she'd rather talk to you alone first."

"Don't be ridiculous. You were the one who got me here. We'll both sit and lap up compliments."

Adele put her arm around Lucy's shoulders and hugged her impulsively. "You're a dear." She tapped on the door. No answer. "Probably talking on long distance. We may as well go on in."

As Adele opened the door, the first thing Lucy saw was the back view of a Yoga-slant board with a beringed hand dangling near the bottom.

Lucy murmured, "Don't tell me *she's* in Zen meditation."

Certainly Velanie wasn't talking on the phone; it sat on a squatty little table no higher than a footstool, beside the slant board. To give Adele vicarious courage, Lucy marched in first, saying in a clear voice, "Velanie, we just stopped by on our way to lunch."

Still no sound. Lucy was beginning to be irritated all over again: this was carrying Zen too damn far. She went straight to the slant board and walked around it.

Velanie wasn't in any ten-minute meditation. She was totally, horribly dead. Blood oozed from the bashed-in skull and had splashed over the weird white mask covering most of her face. After one sickening look, Lucy stumbled back and groped her way to a chair.

"What—what is it?" Adele said. "Is she sick? I'll call the nurse."

Lucy, about to put her head down between her knees to

stop the waves of dizziness, roused instantly. "Don't touch anything. We'll call the police from another phone." And Sergeant Terrizi will get the inspector. The thought steadied her.

Somebody had to be steady. Adele, after one glance at the corpse, was sobbing wildly. Between sobs, she moaned, "She was so good to me. What will I do now?"

A bell clanged abruptly.

"Oh—that's the timer." Adele bent down to the low table and switched something off. "That means it's time to peel off her beauty mask."

6

SERGEANT TERRIZI'S FACE, usually the ruddy color of terra-cotta, was more like grayish clay when he came out of Velanie's office. Two fingerprint men were still inside, doing what Lucy had once described as dusting backward. The police photographer, the last to arrive, was lighting up the ugly scene with flash cubes. And the police doctor had just left, after delivering what Sergeant Terrizi considered an unnecessarily flip, if nonofficial, summing-up: "Bashed from behind by a dumbbell while head over heels."

Terrizi had promised to report to Lucy as soon as possible, but he decided to wait till after Inspector McDougal arrived and let McDougal handle that job. By nature, the sergeant was a traditionalist; in the several murder cases he'd worked on, the inspector had examined the body and given out as much information as he considered wise, or palatable, or both. And Terrizi wanted things to go on that way.

He also wanted to take the seltzer tablet recommended on television commercials as crumbling instantly in the stomach. But he had no tablet of that sort or any other sort (his mother often said approvingly he had the digestion of a goat), and he thought it would be unsuitable to ask a member of the spa's staff for something to settle his heaving insides.

This was the ugliest killing he'd ever seen in broad daylight, and without the inspector. He was young enough to dread letting anybody know how much it had churned him up. Air, he thought. What I need is air.

He started down the back corridor and was about to turn left into the main hall when a bony female in a red uniform bore down on him. "Sergeant Treezi?" It was obviously a rhetorical question; she already knew who he was even if her pronunciation was somewhat elliptical. "Mrs. Ramsdale sent me to show you the way."

He tried to make firm, official-sounding excuses, but in his weakened state he retrogressed: at the age of fourteen, he had been the Ramsdales' yard boy, with grimy hands and green thumbs, and whenever Lucy had said, in effect, "Come here, Nicky," he had come. Now, feeling the old compulsion to obey, he nodded helplessly and followed the bean pole in the red getup. She led him to the other end of the back corridor, through the open door of a bedroom, and straight on to a small terrace.

Lucy sat at a long table in front of a thermos and a tray piled with sandwiches swaddled in Pliofilm. "Thank you, Mavis," she said. "I don't know what I'd do without you. Nicky, sit down in that chaise. Have a little black coffee first"—she didn't say, "to settle your stomach," but that comforting thought came across. "And then we'll eat. I had the kitchen make us some roast-beef sandwiches."

To Mavis, she said, "Sergeant Terrizi has been handling the preliminaries in this murder investigation, and he needs to keep up his strength. The inspector relies on him a great deal."

As Mavis, cow-eyed with admiration, brought him his cup of black coffee, Terrizi began to feel better even before the first sip. Some portion of his mind was aware that Lucy was laying it on thick, but this was one of those times when extravagant praise was the restorative he needed.

Even after the maid had been tactfully got rid of, Lucy didn't push; she poured more coffee, handed over a plate of sandwiches, and they ate in companionable silence, broken only by the sound of munching, and Lucy's occasional murmurs: "I must get the recipe for this bread from the assistant chef . . . he bakes it himself. . . . Have another . . . more coffee?"

The sergeant knew it couldn't last; he had known Lucy Ramsdale too long to be deceived on that. But right now he was soothed and grateful. His eyes, which had been glazed over, were once more like shiny black olives. Ruddiness was coming back to his nice young face. He had finished a second sandwich, and accepted a third cup of coffee, when an odd noise—a combination of clucks and whizzy ticks—surprised his ears. When he saw the helicopter settle down on the side lawn twenty feet away, he was in the state once described by a clever Greek as "suspension of disbelief." It seemed right and natural that Inspector McDougal should step out, wave the giant bird aloft again, and walk—stride, really—across the grass to the terrace. It also seemed right and natural that the inspector looked first at Lucy. "You all right?"

Lucy's eyes were so glistening she might have been near tears, but all she said was "I'm glad you're here." It sounded like a simple statement, but somehow the words hung in the air.

Sergeant Terrizi didn't resent her statement; he was glad himself. He had never handled a murder investigation all

94

on his own and he had no overweening desire to do it just yet. His friend and mentor, the inspector, was still much better at the job.

Lucy was pouring coffee into a third cup. "Nicky came by to tell me what the police doctor said." (Terrizi thought indignantly, You mean you had me dragged in here.) Lucy went on, "And I insisted he stay long enough to have a sandwich." The sergeant stopped feeling cross; she had taken full responsibility. "You'd better have a sandwich yourself while he's filling you in. It will save time. And afterward I can give you some background on the people involved. It's lucky I came here when I did."

The last sentence was so typically Lucy-like that McDougal was reassured.

He had been at a demonstration in the basement shooting range of the New York Police Academy when he'd been paged to take the call from Wingate's Chief of Police Salter. The chief had been forcible but not terribly clear. Mrs. Ramsdale had phoned them ten minutes before about a killing. "She's staying there at that reducing place, God only knows why. Probably read in the tea leaves a killer might strike on Thursday, so she moves in on Wednesday and finds the body on schedule. Owner of the spa, the cosmetic dame Madame Velanie. Rich as an Arab oil sheik—big stuff. We'll have the press on our necks the minute they get a whiff of this."

The chief said he'd already sent Sergeant Terrizi, the police doctor, and technicians, and had called the state police in Hartford to ask Hanson to send more men. "And Hanson told me how to get hold of you in New York." The chief hadn't asked if retired Inspector McDougal would head the investigation. He had taken that for granted: if Lucy Ramsdale was already entangled, would the inspector hang loose? The chief's only worry, a fretful one, was how long it would take McDougal to drive the fifty-some miles from New York. "They started work again yesterday on that stretch from Danbury to Wingate, and you may have to detour to hell and gone around it." McDougal said he'd leave right away and get there as soon as he could.

Fortunately, for him at least, the wife of the police chief in neighboring Ridgefield, Connecticut, had just broken her hip while canning. "Crawled up on a counter to reach for the sterilizer on the top shelf," the husband explained tersely. "If I've told her once . . ."

The unfortunate woman had been rushed to the Wingate Hospital for emergency surgery, and a helicopter belonging to Fairfield County was now on its way to pick up her husband on the launching pad at the foot of Wall Street. He would be glad to give McDougal a lift by air and drop him off in Wingate. And one of his detectives who was staying on for the afternoon session would drive McDougal's car home later that day.

They had been whizzed in a police car, courtesy of New York's finest, to the launching pad, and were aloft by one-fifteen. There hadn't been time for lunch, and even if there had been, McDougal wouldn't have felt like chewing and swallowing. Not till he'd checked on Lucy.

Now he bit into a roast-beef sandwich with good appetite, and drank remarkably good coffee. Lucy was O.K. Still rather pale, but O.K. He didn't resent, as he sometimes did, her coming in on a gory murder like a bee gathering honey. It would help her get over the shock of finding the body.

The sergeant was being restrained in his description of the corpse and the murder weapon, but McDougal could read between the bare words and supply his own adjectives.

". . . found in her office lying upside down on a tilted board."

"Yoga," Lucy put in. "You put your feet over your head to get more blood into your brain and think beautiful thoughts." Her lips suddenly quivered, and her hand holding a coffee cup shook so hard the cup clattered on the saucer. "I hope she was. I hope she didn't even know."

"She would have died instantly." McDougal wasn't at all sure this was true, but if it comforted Lucy, and he could see it did, then that was good enough for now. She wouldn't read the pathologist's report.

Terrizi said he'd already sent the dumbbell to the lab to see if they could bring up latent fingerprints on a weapon that had been wiped clean.

"Can you imagine killing somebody with a dumbbell?" Lucy was obviously feeling better. "It seems so ludicrously old-fashioned. Velanie kept them all over the place, like matches or something. One in the office and one in the cottage. She probably bought them by the gross, she had so many houses."

Terrizi ignored this frivolous interruption. He said that the victim was wearing several valuable rings and a brooch (he pronounced the double "o" as in "brood"), so robbery wasn't the motive. Her handbag, found in the top desk drawer, contained several hundred dollars in cash. Death had occurred between approximately twelve-thirty and twelve-forty. Madame Velanie had called both Mrs. Ramsdale and the publicity woman, Mrs. Vining, around twelve-thirty. The switchboard had no record of in-house calls, so the exact time to the minute couldn't be determined.

97

Lucy said, "I know it was close to twelve-thirty because I was beginning to feel starved and I wanted lunch."

It had always amused and amazed the inspector that so small and delicately built a woman could get ravenously hungry and pack away the amount of food she did.

"Velanie wanted us to come over to her office right then because she was crazy about a sketch I'd done this morning. And she wanted to have new exercise suits made from my design. I'd jazzed them up in the sketch so they were much more attractive."

Unlike the sergeant, McDougal didn't mind her adding a few unnecessary and egocentric details. It meant she was back to normal. In his relaxed state, he did something he almost never did—made a small joke. "So Velanie's accountant didn't want her to spend money on new exercise suits and he killed her to keep down the overhead."

Unconsciously, he was waiting to hear Lucy's delicious laugh. She usually laughed at his jokes, even the feeble ones, as if she were encouraging a too sober child. But now she only stared at him. "You already know about Arnold Wynn? You're amazing."

The inspector would have liked to wear this laurel, however undeserved it might be, but it felt prickly. Quite apart from his need to get the whole story, his conscience made him admit ignorance, and Lucy enjoyed filling him in. She described Arnold Wynn, ex-husband, ex-head accountant of Velanie, Incorporated, and gave highlights of her ride with him the evening before. "And this morning around nine Wynn was in Velanie's office telling her about Celia and Jason—that's Velanie's husband—having an affair. She didn't sound as if she believed him—she was yelling at him. In a way I don't blame her. Wynn drinks like a sponge. But he got her started in the business and helped build it up to a huge corporation and now he doesn't even own any stock." She gave them Wynn's account of how Velanie had taken his stock in exchange for a few thousand dollars to pay off some woman. "But I still think he should have been left with something. After all, Velanie was worth millions, so he had reason to feel bitter. And he must be down in her will."

Terrizi didn't like the way the ball was rolling—or, rather, the way Mrs. Ramsdale was rolling it. "Wynn seemed really broken up when he heard she was dead. He insisted on coming in to look at the body, and he cried."

"Well, if he'd just killed her, he couldn't very well burst out laughing."

The sergeant ran his hand through his springy black curls and counted to nine before he continued. "Wynn kept saying, 'Vellie, Vellie.' And he said, 'She would have wanted to look handsome for her funeral and now she's a mess.' Then he cried some more."

"Poor old thing." Lucy's sympathies had already shifted. "I don't really think he had the nerve to kill her. And if he had, he'd have done it decently so she'd look all right afterward."

Terrizi said, "For my money, it's the husband." He hadn't taken to Jason. The bereaved husband had been summoned to view the body and had promptly stumbled over to the window and vomited into the planter. As the son of Mrs. Terrizi, a compulsive cleaner who often made her family take their shoes off at the door, the sergeant had found this reaction of Jason's inexcusably messy. The guy could have rushed to the bathroom. At the very least, he should have aimed at the office wastebasket.

The sergeant tried to think of a delicate way to say this in front of Lucy—that a man who throws up all over a

99

planter is not a stable character and might well kill some-body impulsively and then be sorry. He decided to mention it later when he got the inspector alone; he hoped that would be any minute now.

Lucy was already offering up a substitute for the role of First Murderer. "Celia's much more the type."

The inspector thought, Who is Celia? and realized it sounded like a sixteenth-century verse: "Who is Celia? what is she? / That she would bash a la-dy?"

Lucy was still expounding: ". . . and if Arnold Wynn finally convinced Velanie her husband was playing around with that girl— Oh, that must be why Celia came to the pool to get Jason."

Now that Celia began to sound important, McDougal wanted to get her straight. He made Lucy backtrack, which she did impatiently, with an air of *If you'd been listening in the first place* . . . Celia Grant was the manager of the spa. She had gone to work for Velanie as a gauche young girl, and Velanie had practically adopted her and not only trained her but showed her how to make the most of her looks. "Of course her legs must have been all right to start with. And she's pretty enough, if you like the candy-box-cover sort."

It wasn't at all hard to guess, from Lucy's tone, what she thought of the candy-box-cover kind of looks. "She was such a pet of Velanie's she even took lots of business trips with her, to Europe and so on. But then Jason came along."

"From where?"

"One of those gyms in New York. That's where Velanie saw him when she was hiring staff for the spa. He'd been an Olympic diving champion and he should have been able to cash in on that and be in Grade B movies or something. He's quite good-looking. In fact, I wanted to sketch him. That's why I went to the pool this morning for his class, but Celia got there first and was all over him in front of those women."

McDougal began to feel Lucy was being too scattery. He said with mild sarcasm, "Were he and Celia making love under water to demonstrate to the class?"

Lucy gave a hoot of laughter. She had suddenly remembered a time in Key West, on the beach with her husband, when they'd seen a young couple thrashing around wildly, mostly under water, but surfacing occasionally, still entwined, to get air, then submerging again. There had been no doubt whatsoever about what they were doing. Hal had quoted a line from an old Cole Porter song: "Goldfish in the privacy of bowls do it." He'd said, "You'll have to admit this is at least more private than a goldfish bowl." She was still laughing when she saw that Terrizi and McDougal were looking at her worriedly.

"I just meant Celia was hanging on to him and she'd been crying and she took him away when the class had barely started."

"This Wynn, the ex-husband, could have made up the whole story about their sleeping together." Terrizi's lower lip was sticking out. He had been very favorably impressed with Celia Grant. When she saw the body, she hadn't sobbed or screamed. She had turned very white and looked as if she might faint, but she had pulled herself together almost instantly, to answer questions. She said she'd had lunch alone in her cottage, as she often did, to get some special work done. And she had taken at least one phone call during that time.

"That's what *she* says. Make her prove it."

"We'll check it later. Go on, Terrizi. What else?"

When Celia Grant didn't eat in her cottage, she ate with the guests in the main dining room. She and five of the instructors took turns on this, two at a meal. "Miss Grant gave me a list of the staff, and she was very concerned about the instructors. She asked permission to go break the news to them herself."

Terrizi had been touched by her concern. Unlike the publicity woman, Mrs. Vining, who had been in the infirmary ever since he arrived, Miss Grant was a person to count on in an emergency. She hadn't struck him as the sort who would sleep with the husband of an employer she'd been devoted to.

McDougal said, "And where was the husband, Jason, during that twelve-thirty to twelve-forty period?"

"Soon as I asked him, he threw up again. I had to let him go clean himself up, but I thought you'd want to interview him yourself, considering he's the likeliest of the lot."

Lucy's temper fizzed. "He's a damn sight more honest than Celia. And I know they were having an affair, because he told me so himself last night. He was with me when you phoned, Mac. He said Celia resented Velanie marrying again and would hardly speak to him, so just for fun he made a play for her and she fell like a ton of hot bricks. A reformed virgin always goes overboard. She even wanted to marry him 'after Velanie is gone.' But Jason was already sick of her and he was scared his wife would find out. And I'll bet she did—Velanie, I mean. Probably she soon believed what Wynn was telling her and called Celia in and raised hell, so Celia grabbed the dumbbell and let her have it. Then she went to the pool to tell Jason what she'd done."

As Lucy's top-of-the-head words echoed back to her, she

102

had to renege on some of them instantly. "Velanie couldn't have been dead when Celia went to the pool, because it was only a little after eleven-thirty then and Velanie called Adele and me much later. I already told you—around twelve-thirty."

"You're positive it was Velanie on the phone?"

"Of course I am." Lucy sat up very straight, giving off righteous rays. "You know how my ears are."

The inspector knew: a fox would be lucky to have them.

"Velanie was sounding a bit foggy but that was because of the mask."

"The mask!"

"Skin stuff you spread on and leave till it smooths out wrinkles." Terrizi's tone indicated considerable skepticism. "It was hard as a rock. The doctor practically had to crack it with a hammer to get it off."

"The timer went off just after we found her, and it was already hard then, but it shouldn't have been. It's supposed to peel off. Nicky, get me that Wrinkles Away cream from the dressing table."

The sergeant might have resented being called Nicky and sent to fetch like the yard boy of ten years before, but he had seen the inspector's face go tense with a look that was unmistakable: like a bloodhound getting the scent or an ordinary dog smelling raw beef. The mask was important. Something about the timing . . . In the welter of bottles and jars on the dressing table, he found the right one and hurried back with it to the terrace. He would have handed it to McDougal but Lucy snatched it out of his hand.

"Let's see . . . 'Do not use if allergic to—' Hell, being allergic wouldn't have bashed her head in." She was reading down the directions on the back of the bottle. " 'If skin is sensitive, remove early.' When is early? Oh, here: 'For normal skins, twenty minutes. Peel off in one piece, starting at the top . . .' " She waved the jar triumphantly. "So it's not supposed to be like cement, because you couldn't peel off cement. Somebody must have reset the timer." She had a sudden recollection of Adele Vining urging her to hurry.

"What about the publicity woman who went to Velanie's office with you?" The inspector was picking Lucy's thoughts as easily as if he were plucking watercress. He was used to reading her face, which was not the sort described as "poker." "The reset timer would give her an alibi."

"That's impossible," Lucy said hotly. "I've known Adele Vining for years."

McDougal's lips twitched; he had heard that before. Lucy saw his amusement, and flung herself into the defense. "Adele couldn't have done it in the four or five minutes after Velanie called me. That's as long as it was before Adele came to get me." As Lucy remembered details more clearly, she felt calm and reassured. "And Adele is the last person who'd do it. Velanie gave her ten thousand dollars right out, as a present, to pay for treatment her husband will have in Zurich. And the sooner he has it, the better. Poor Adele's all on edge. She got an SOS summons from Celia Grant's office right after she'd taken me down to see the work sessions this morning. Something about a phone call. I know she thought the nursing home was trying to reach her because Lewis was worse again. She looked ghastly, and rushed right off. I was relieved when she told me later it was only only *Harper's Bazaar* calling about a photograph." Lucy sniffed. "Magazine people and their emergencies."

McDougal was still thinking about the ten thousand dollars. "Maybe the money was blackmail, and Velanie had no choice but to pay it, and she drew the line at paying more."

"Would Adele have told me about it if it was blackmail? That's ridiculous."

The inspector decided to check on this with somebody less biased. "How about Velanie's secretary?" he asked Terrizi. "Did she know about that ten thousand?"

The sergeant looked stricken. He not only hadn't talked to a secretary; in all the confusion, he hadn't even missed her. He gulped painfully, almost swallowing his Adam's apple in the process, and admitted his sin of omission.

The inspector's long, bony face was stern in disapproval.

"I was—uh—busy with the preliminaries and I haven't really interviewed anybody yet. I was waiting till—"

"You should have got on to it right away, before they had a chance to cook up their alibis." He looked at the empty plate and coffee cup on the small wrought-iron table beside Terrizi and his expression could have meant *Picnicking here while a murderer's on the loose.*

The sergeant was mortified; Lucy saw his expression. "Mac, you're being unfair," she said furiously. "If you'd stayed home in the first place, instead of going off to some stupid convention . . . Nicky's been doing your work, and now that you're finally here I don't see *you* rushing off to interview people right and left. You drop down out of the skies like Superman and sit here criticizing everybody else, when we've been through a horrible time. Nicky had to see that body—that hideous sight—on an empty stomach. And he stayed on and on in that office—"

She made it sound like "The boy stood on the burning deck, / Whence all but he had fled." She was about to elaborate on the sergeant's selfless performance when a new thought struck her. "And the secretary wasn't around anyway. Her office is next to Velanie's and I took Adele in there right away to calm her down. I called the police from that phone. My God, you don't suppose the secretary's been killed, too?"

"If you didn't find another body, it's not likely." McDougal enjoyed seeing Lucy in fighting form. And he thought she was more right than wrong on Terrizi. He'd been heavy-handed with the youngster, and he himself had taken time to have a sandwich. He could just as well have gone straight to the corpse and been briefed on the spot. It wouldn't have been the first time he'd gone without lunch. Even to himself he wouldn't admit that Lucy's shining pleasure in his arrival had made him linger.

Apologizing was always difficult for him, but he did it now, indirectly. "You had your hands full," he said to Terrizi. "And it probably didn't hurt to postpone any real interviewing till the"—he started to say "suspects" but amended it—"husband and ex-husband and Miss Grant are in better condition to talk. But it's odd about the secretary not being around. What's her name?"

Terrizi pulled the list of staff people out of his pocket and consulted it with every show of efficiency. "Simms, Hilda. She may have taken a long lunch hour."

"For two and a half hours!" Lucy's eyebrows expressed derision. "Velanie would never put up with it. She worked that woman like a slave."

"Then why isn't the secretary around when she's needed?" The inspector, having been somewhat derelict in his own performance of duty, resented it all the more in the missing Hilda Simms. "If her office was right next door to Velanie's, she'd have been more apt to hear something. We'd better get on it right away." He stood up, all six feet three inches of him. "Sergeant, ask Miss Grant what room we can use for interviews."

"If Adele's still in the infirmary," Lucy said, "you could work in her office. It's next to the secretary's. I'll call the nurse and find out how she is."

But Adele wasn't in the infirmary. The nurse reported that Mrs. Vining had insisted on going back to her office. "She said she had to call the TV stations right away, so they could get it on the evening news."

The inspector and Terrizi waited impatiently for Lucy to hang up and report. She did this with admirable brevity, although a certain subjective coloration crept in. "Adele's back in her office because she wanted to call the networks and everybody about Velanie. She's so conscientious, poor dear. All she'd take was a Valium and a cup of tea."

Terrizi said he'd find Miss Grant and then meet Mc-Dougal in Velanie's office. He gave the inspector directions: "Straight down this back corridor, last door on your left. The fingerprint men and photographer are still working there."

As soon as he'd said it, he had an awful thought: he had told the men he'd be gone only a few minutes. What if they'd finished and cleared out, and left the place unlocked, wide open for the murderer to sneak in and maybe remove incriminating evidence? He mumbled, "See you," and bolted.

Lucy was annoyed that he hadn't even said "thank you for lunch," but she decided he was being hyper-efficient to make up for his earlier lapse.

The inspector was already calling the state police barracks. Afterward he thanked Lucy for the sandwich and said, "Take care of yourself." But he still didn't go.

Lucy often rode her intuition like a broomstick, and this was one of those times: she sensed he needed another helping of thanks himself. "When you stepped out of that helicopter, I felt as if you'd come just in time to pull me out of a swamp."

McDougal gave her one of his rare smiles, and the change in his face was extraordinary, as if a tightly shuttered window had been opened to the sun. "Thank the cop's wife who broke her hip. We ought to go see her sometime in the hospital."

Coming from McDougal, it was an astonishingly outgoing suggestion.

"We'll go as soon as you finish this case." *With my help* was generously left unsaid.

But at the door, Lucy rather spoiled this by adding, "Isn't it lucky I'm right here on the spot? I can work from the inside."

"Within limits."

She knew he was warning her again to be careful. Even while she said, "Of course," her face was bright with anticipation.

McDougal had his hand on the doorknob when the knock came; he jerked back in reflex, then reached to open the door.

"Inspector McDougal?" The woman's face was blotchy from crying, and her brown wig had slid up on one side to show the gray hair underneath, but her voice was controlled. "I'm Madame Velanie's secretary, Hilda Simms. Marta Galt told me where to find you."

"Oh, God," Lucy said to McDougal. "That television woman. She must have seen the helicopter land and she recognized you. I'll go find out what she's up to." She patted Hilda's arm. "I'm so terribly sorry you had such a shock. Mrs. Vining told me you'd been with Velanie over twenty years."

The secretary's surface composure cracked. "If only Madame hadn't sent me to Wingate, she'd still be alive. Nobody would have dared . . . I went to the Inn—the Oaks—but all I could learn was the woman's name. She went out before I got there and I waited over two hours but she didn't come back."

"What woman?" the inspector said.

"A Mrs. Torrance."

McDougal's jaw nearly came unhinged. He had forgotten his ex-wife was even in Wingate.

7

IN HIS HASTE to get back to the corpse, Sergeant Terrizi nearly ran down two women who were coming out of the room next to Lucy's. Both of them wore shapeless, faded red gym suits that looked to him like outsize long underwear, and both had grease smeared all over their faces. Even in the dim light of the corridor, their skins had an almost phosphorescent gleam.

Terrizi muttered an apology and tried to rush on, but the taller of the two women grabbed his arm. "Officer, you *are* here to investigate the murder of Madame Velanie, are you not?"

The sergeant said he was. The woman had a stomach protruding like a kangaroo pouch, and what he thought of as a fancy British accent. He didn't hold the accent against her; he simply hoped she had something concrete to offer in the way of evidence. "If you saw anything you think might be helpful," he began, when she blew that hope to shreds: "Sorry, we were all in the dining room from twelve-fifteen till just after one, and Marta Galt said the killing took place during that time."

Marta Galt, the television woman. How had she got hold of the news so soon? Even to having the time of the murder.

Sergeant Terrizi squared his shoulders and used his sternest official voice. "Did one of you call her at the network?"

Fancy-accent looked puzzled. "Why should we? She's here at the spa. She has the room right above Mrs. Ramsdale's."

Terrizi cursed silently, and with feeling. If Marta Galt had been at her window over Lucy's terrace listening to their conversation, she might report everything on her program and then all hell would break loose.

"This is still confidential information—the time the murder was committed. I must ask you not to tell anybody else." Even as he finished saying it, he thought, That'll just make 'em blab all the more.

"Everybody already knows," the shorter woman said. She had a shiny moon face and hair like mildewed hay. "Marta came down to the lounge and told us the news a while ago."

"What exactly did she tell you?"

"Just that Madame Velanie had been murdered while we were having lunch."

Terrizi let out a whoosh of relief. The Galt woman must have heard plenty more than that when she eavesdropped.

Hay-hair said, "I nearly upchucked my lunch when Marta told us."

Fancy-accent laughed throatily. "Oh, nonsense. It's too long a time till dinner."

"If we're still here then."

"That's what I wanted to ask you about, Officer. Will

111

there be some of you here at night now? If we stay on, we'd like to be sure we're adequately protected."

Terrizi said he thought there would be at least two men on night duty. He was too cautious to promise blanket safety.

The shorter woman said breathily that two didn't sound like much. "In murder mysteries, they keep a cop outside a bedroom door all night."

"Only if the person inside is a suspect," her friend said with authority. "Do stop fussing, Marilyn. You may sleep in my room if you're nervous. We can't go home now and miss all the excitement. We'll dine out on this story for weeks. Thank you, Officer, you've been very helpful. Come, Marilyn, time for our pore pack."

She swept her friend off down the corridor, and Terrizi, not wanting to be stuck with them again, waited till they'd disappeared. This time he covered at least ten feet before another door opened. He was about to rush past when he saw who it was: Celia Grant. She had changed to a sleeveless black dress, and although it didn't show off her legs as generously, the sergeant approved of this sign of mourning.

"Oh, Sergeant, I was just going to look for you. Do you think we should send the clients home and close the spa while the investigation is going on? I didn't want to decide anything till I'd consulted you."

There is nothing more mellowing than to be consulted by a well-stacked woman.

The sergeant threw caution over his left shoulder and said that as far as he knew they could carry on.

"Oh, thank you. It's what Madame would have wanted."

This mention of Madame reminded Terrizi forcibly that

112

he'd better get back to her office. "Is there a room the inspector could use for interviews?" As soon as he'd said it, he wished he'd said "the inspector and I."

Celia Grant wasn't the sort who searched up and down her mind looking for answers; she knew instantly. "The dietitian is on vacation this week. You may use her office if you don't mind some noise from the kitchen."

At home, the sergeant ate in the kitchen except on special occasions, and a quiet kitchen would have given him the quivers. It would have meant that his voluble mother, and in fact the whole family, was sick. He said the dietitian's office would be fine.

"I'll take you there right now." Her tone was suddenly brisk.

When Terrizi said he couldn't go until later, he saw Celia Grant's lips press together pinchily, and realized she was annoyed. Why? Did she want him deflected from Velanie's corpse for a while?

She gave him overly detailed directions for finding the dietitian's office, and instead of being grateful, he thought, She's bossy. And she thinks I'm not very bright.

As he went on down the corridor, he thought with contentment that his Angie had legs as good as Miss Grant's or better. And Angie was never bossy. At least, not so's you could notice it. She got her own way nine times out of ten, but she made you feel good about it.

The police photographer, a middle-aged man with a bald dome and a mangy mustache, was the only one left in Madame Velanie's office. Instead of complaining about Terrizi's "few minutes" absence being more like forty minutes, he waved aside the sergeant's explanation with an absentminded flick of one hand. The other hand was touching—caressing—a large, square, starkly modern electric clock that sat on the desk. "Always wanted to see one of these things," he said dreamily. "Want to know what time it is in Bangkok?"

Terrizi really didn't want to know what time it was in Bangkok, but he owed the photographer a return courtesy for having stuck around with the corpse. The body, which had been moved to a chaise longue, was decently covered with a sheet, and the place looked as it had when Terrizi left, except that the wastebasket was half full of used flash cubes, and the fingerprint men had left smudges of dusting powder around. "Sure, what time is it in Bangkok?" He tried to sound eager.

The photographer studied his new plaything, or communed with it, and said triumphantly, "Three o'clock tomorrow morning."

"It's later than I thought."

"And in Vladivostok—" The photographer broke off abruptly as McDougal came into the room. "Just finishing up here, Inspector. I'll have prints for you by—" For a second, he seemed confused by the sudden change in time. "By—uh—six P.M."

McDougal said, "Good," and waited, pointedly, for the photographer to leave. And the photographer, after one last, wistful look at his new love the clock, collected his camera and left.

Instead of going straight to the corpse on the chaise, McDougal said abruptly, "Nicky, I've hit a complication."

Terrizi was surprised. The inspector almost never called him Nicky while they were working on a case. And if there'd been complications before, as there frequently had been, McDougal never called them that. He'd simply taken them as they came and solved them.

"My ex-wife has been missing all day, and the secretary thinks she came out here and killed Velanie."

114

Terrizi was too flabbergasted to speak. How had the inspector's ex-wife got into this?

"It's ridiculous, of course, but we'd better track her down and get things straightened out right away. Try the hairdressers in Wingate first. Thursday used to be her day for hair and all that."

"Yes, sir. If you could—well, if you'd give me a description of her." He hesitated, not wanting to add, "And her current married name," because he thought it might still be a painful point, but he had to say it.

The inspector looked surprised at the question. "Mrs. Torrance. You saw her yesterday at headquarters."

Terrizi did well not to say, Jeez, you mean *her*. He said, with restraint, "I'll get right on it."

With that taken care of, or at least under way, the inspector was ready to pull back the sheet and look at the body.

"Funny she didn't use her hands to protect her head from the blows. The hands don't show any mark at all. First blow must have been from behind, coming down hard enough to stun her. And after that . . ."

It wasn't a pretty idea to contemplate. No prettier than the battered head of the corpse. The Yoga board was still near the desk, with splotches of blood at the bottom. The sergeant saw McDougal stare at this, frowning, and was happy to explain. "That's where her head was. They lie upside down on the thing." Terrizi was thankful he'd asked Celia Grant about this when she'd first seen the body. "So more blood goes to the head and makes them calm or something."

"She's calm all right now. Kind of Procrustean—try to knock off her head to make her fit."

The sergeant made a mental note of "Procrustean," so that he could look it up in the *Columbia Encyclopedia*

Angie had given him for Christmas after he'd hinted he'd much prefer it to a watch that could swim under water. His vocabulary had stretched tremendously since he'd started working with the inspector.

McDougal took a handkerchief out of his pocket, wrapped it around his hand, and picked up the timer from the low table beside the Yoga board. "If this was reset to establish an alibi, there's a chance we might get a print from it. The lab men should have taken it along with the dumbbell." Terrizi said he'd drop it off, and nearly added, "On my way in to locate your ex-wife," but swallowed the words in time.

The office was almost as large as Lucy's room at the other end of the corridor, but without a terrace. As a substitute touch, there were several massive plants—two cacti and a philodendron—in a long planter set against the French doors. "Certainly nobody got in that way."

Except for the planter and the chaise, the office furnishings seemed to be not only utilitarian but mostly on the cheap side. There were two muddy-green filing cabinets along the far wall, a small table the phone sat on beside the Yoga board, and three unprepossessing chairs, including the one behind the desk. The desk itself was mahogany and the most modern piece in the room: the outsize green blotter covering two-thirds of the top looked somehow incongruous. All the more so in contrast to the photograph of the dead woman at the back of the desk: it looked as if she were about to be presented at court—elaborately bejeweled and brocaded.

"She doesn't look like the type who'd have yogurt and an apple for lunch," Terrizi said. "But that's all there was in the fridge here, and a maid said that's what Velanie usually ate. From what Mama told me, she sure made up for it at dinner."

116

McDougal glanced at the photograph of the dead woman, which stared back at him—imperious, demanding, so different from the battered corpse that he found himself saying to it silently, "We'll get the answers."

He asked Terrizi to stay there till the body was collected. "Probably another fifteen or twenty minutes. The barracks will send along a state cop who'll take over and stand guard till we get this place locked up. Velanie's secretary just came back from town and I don't want to talk to her in her office." He indicated the door in the side wall. "She's already upset enough, and she shouldn't be around when they take out the body. Did you arrange for a room we can use?"

Terrizi was glad to have a solid answer to that one. He gave directions for finding the dietitian's office. "The side hall runs at right angle to this back one, and the dietitian's office opens off that, first door on your right. Miss Grant said there might be some noise from the kitchen." As McDougal got to the door, the sergeant blurted out something that was still worrying him. "Marta Galt, the TV woman, has the room right above Mrs. Ramsdale's, and she must have listened when the three of us were talking on the terrace." He repeated what the two women with greasy faces had told him. "What if she decides to use a lot more than that on her program?"

"Lucy's going to muzzle her," the inspector said mildly. "Good luck on tracking down Mrs. Torrance."

After his idol had gone, Terrizi re-covered the corpse, carefully not looking any more than he had to, but fortified by a cheering interior monologue: The inspector's not at all the way he was when his ex-wife came back from Europe a while ago. Now he's annoyed she turned up, but that's all.

The sergeant had up-and-down feelings about Mrs.

Ramsdale, but at the moment he was strongly up. She had given the inspector what seemed to be immunity from the former Mrs. McDougal, and for that Terrizi blessed her.

There was no noise at all in the dietitian's small office. Not even the far-off clatter of a pan from the kitchen two doors away. McDougal arranged his long legs under the too-low desk, and called Lucy's room to ask her to send Hilda Simms to the dietitian's office.

"Dietitian! Are you getting the lowdown on how to lose weight?"

The inspector, a bony hundred-and-fifty-pounder, explained a bit stiffly he was using the vacationing dietitian's office for interviews.

Lucy said that Hilda Simms was having a sandwich on the terrace, "But she'll be along in five or ten minutes."

McDougal suspected more than a sandwich was involved, but he couldn't very well say, "Don't you pump her." Anyway, Hilda Simms wouldn't know who Mrs. Torrance was, and neither did Lucy. He preferred it that way. Terrizi would soon find out in Wingate what Eileen had been up to. Her ex-husband hoped fervently it was something as harmless as having her hair dyed magenta.

While he was waiting for the secretary, he studied the memo board hanging on the wall beside the desk. Some of the notes scrawled in red pencil seemed to be lists of ingredients. Recipes? McDougal had always had a weakness for cookbooks. (Mrs. Beeton, 1896 edition, was one of his favorites, which he'd picked up for fifty cents at the Wingate Thrift Shop.) He wasn't a gourmet cook; his specialties were steaks and chops, but he was like the armchair traveler who enjoys reading of far-off places as long as he doesn't have to go there.

118

He couldn't resist reading one of the slips tacked to the memo board:

Add sesame seeds and mung to chopped spinach!

He should have stopped there, but the stuff had a horrid fascination.

Hors d'oeuvres—nonfat cottage cheese with grated alfalfa sprouts, ginger, and half cup sushi raw fish. Serve on unsalted Melba with *cocktail* of brewers' yeast in tomato juice. Call it an Unbloody Mary!

E.M.F. diet? Month without food is *too long*.

Mousse: 8 bunches watercress
       1 cup salted water
       2 tsps. vinegar
       Cook watercress till wilted. Drain, puree with vinegar, serve.
       NO CALORIES!

The inspector's digestive juices curdled; when the knock came at the door, he was so relieved he almost shouted, "Come in."

What appeared was so unexpected that he sat staring dumbly: a small man of around thirty, non-Caucasian, probably Japanese, with long black hair to his shoulders, contained in a kind of red fishnet. This apparition wore a starched white tunic over dungarees and it crackled as he bowed.

"Inspector? I am Chef Ronda. Miss Grant ask me to report to you where my staff is for hour from noon to one, runchtime today. Everyone in kitchen entire hour. Not even go to ravatory. They ate in kitchen after guests finished runch."

The "runch" and "ravatory" reminded McDougal of a

Japanese classmate of his in Harvard, years before, singing a new hit song: "Farring in Ruv with Ruv."

He said, "Thank you. I'm glad to have that straight. And all the guests were in the dining room during that time, so it cuts down our lists of suspects considerably."

His odd-looking visitor, instead of bowing and backing out, said unexpectedly, "You think of every chef as fat, jorry-rooking man in tarr white hat. That's ord stuff. Newest trend in cooking is row choresteror. No butter, cream, rich seasonings. We find piquant substitutes and use many nature foods. Very good for reducing spa."

"Have you been working for Madame long?" McDougal nearly said "rong."

"I train in Switzerrand, then in Paris under famous diet chef Madame Veranie know. When she pran to open this reducing spa, she ask his advice and he recommend me. Madame so happy with my work here she say she take me soon to be her own chef in New York. But even before her death, I decide not. She roozes temper too easy."

It was beginning to sound interesting. McDougal was about to say, "Sit down, won't you?" when Ronda said, "If you excuse me, I must go prepare very marverous dinner to take radies' minds off murder."

He had just bowed his way out when Hilda Simms arrived. She looked considerably better now, with wig on straight, nose powdered although her eyelids were still blotchy, and even fresh lipstick. The lipstick must have been applied hurriedly; a small streak of red went off at one corner of her mouth, tilting up like a painted-on smile, and McDougal found that touching.

"Madame often sends me—sent me—on confidential errands." The pride in her voice, along with the slight quaver when she changed to the past tense, was touching,

120

too. "She trusted me more than anybody else." Hilda Simms had been Madame's secretary "twenty-three years last June fifth." It might have been her wedding anniversary, the way she said it. When she added, "Through Madame's last three husbands," he thought, at first she was being sarcastic, then realized she was simply giving an example of her own staying power as compared to husbands. "Not that I'd call Jason Pappas a real husband. He's more like an oversexed gigolo. I didn't want Madame to marry him, but it wouldn't have done any good to tell her that. She had a thing about marriage. I mean, for herself. She didn't care what her clients did—sleeping around and all that—but she would never have done it herself. She needed to be respectable. Her first husband, Arnold Wynn, may not seem like much now, but he used to be a very fine accountant. When he's sober, he's still smart. And he knows all the tricks for dodging taxes." She seemed to remember suddenly she was talking to a police officer, and added in a rush, "I mean, without breaking the law."

The inspector couldn't resist saying, "Like whisking a few million into a numbered Swiss bank account? Don't worry, I'm not here to investigate financial shenanigans except as they might apply to murder. Would you say this business is financially sound?"

The secretary relaxed visibly. "Oh, yes! And Madame used two different accounting firms as a double check. And she'd go over the books herself night after night. She didn't sleep more than four or five hours a night, so she often worked then, but she'd take catnaps during the day, even five or ten minutes. She could drop off to sleep anywhere, even in the car."

Or on a Yoga board. It would explain how the killer could have struck the first blow. But it didn't explain why.

121

"Did she consult Arnold Wynn regularly as an accountant and tax expert?"

"Almost never any more. But she got an offer earlier this month from a syndicate—I mean, a group of reputable financiers."

McDougal suppressed a grin. *I didn't think you meant the Mafia.*

"And she wanted Wynn's advice on the best way to handle the deal for taxes, if she decided to go ahead."

"As far as you know, did any of the people close to her—Wynn, Jason, Celia Grant—did any of them oppose the sale to the syndicate?"

She shook her head so vehemently her wig looked as if it were coming unanchored again. "Absolutely not. Celia couldn't have lost her job if the syndicate took over, because Madame had already made that a stipulation. Jason's job is too measly to matter, and Arnold's on an allowance."

She blinked at the inspector's next question but she answered readily enough. Yes, she had heard Madame yelling at Arnold Wynn that morning, and had got enough to guess what it was about.

"Velanie's husband and Celia Grant having an affair. Was that it?"

"That's what Arnold Wynn said, but Madame didn't believe him. She told me so later. She might have believed it about Jason, but not about Celia. She loved that girl. She might yell at the rest of us when she was in one of her tantrums, but hardly ever at Celia."

McDougal heard the cutting edge in the secretary's voice. *She's jealous of Celia having been Velanie's pet.*

"And did *you* think the husband and Celia were having an affair?"

Hilda Simms stared down at her hands. "If they were, it was all his doing," she said slowly, as if she were weighing each word on invisible scales. "Celia's smart about business and she's a good administrator. But she's stayed away from men, maybe because she was afraid of going overboard. So she might have been like the sleeping beauty, but sort of in reverse. When a man finally woke her up, she couldn't help herself. She'd be under a spell."

McDougal was surprised by the analogy: he wouldn't have thought Hilda Simms had that much imagination.

"But Celia wouldn't have given up her job with Madame for anything or anybody," she said.

"You think if Velanie had found out about an affair she'd have fired Miss Grant?"

"I think Madame couldn't let herself believe it. She trusted that girl more than she trusted anybody else except me. And I know she provided for Celia very generously in her will."

McDougal had lit a cigarette absently and now realized there was no ashtray.

"Just dump out the paper clips and use that little bowl."

Hilda Simms didn't miss much, he thought.

"Are you in the will?"

"Madame told me I was. But she's already done so much for me. When my mother got cancer twelve years ago, Madame called in all the best specialists and she paid for an operation and even a private room. And flowers from her greenhouse—her place on Long Island." Hilda Simms spread out her arms. "Bunches this big." Her mouth twisted in a wry smile. "And then she wouldn't give me even a day off for the funeral. Just two hours. But she's like that. I understand. She works incredibly long hours herself, and she expects all of us who work for her to do

123

the same." This time, the secretary didn't seem to notice she'd used the present tense, and McDougal didn't give her time to realize.

"I understand Mrs. Vining's husband is very ill."

If it was an odd non sequitur, his listener supplied an instant connection to what had gone before. "Oh, yes, and Madame found out about a specialist in Zurich and had me write out a big check right away so Mrs. Vining would know they can go ahead and have the treatments and maybe an operation in Zurich."

"You already gave the check to Mrs. Vining?"

"As soon as Madame signed it."

"How recently was that?"

Hilda Simms looked flustered. "I'm sorry. I can't give you the exact date till I get back to my office."

"Just approximately."

"Let's see. Around August seventeenth. I remember because that's Madame's birthday. I gave her a yogurt spoon I found at the Brooklyn Museum, a copy of an antique Turkish spoon, and she was so pleased. She kept it in her office—I mean, in the kitchenette there."

"Did she usually have lunch in her office?"

"Quite often, especially when she wanted to diet. Or when she had to think out a problem."

"Was today a problem day?"

"She was upset about Mrs. Torrance phoning Jason here."

"We're tracking Mrs. Torrance down now. But I frankly doubt if she had anything to do with the killing."

"That's what Mrs. Ramsdale told me after you left. She said your ex-wife is very spoiled and just likes to make mischief."

McDougal nearly choked. How the hell had Lucy guessed? As far as he knew, she'd never heard the name

Torrance. And her summing-up of Eileen, a woman she'd never even met, was uncannily accurate.

"And when I said she probably killed Madame, I was so upset I wasn't even thinking. But I've known people like her. If their luck breaks down, they want to throw tacks in somebody else's path. You're well rid of her, you know. I hope you won't forget that."

The inspector looked at this middle-aged woman with respect. He began to understand why she'd lasted twenty-three years with the mercurial Velanie.

"Thank you," he said. "I won't forget. It shouldn't take us long to find out where she actually was today."

"Have you tried the hairdressers?"

He was so startled he gaped.

"The reason I thought of that—the desk clerk at the Oaks told me Mrs. Torrance is very good-looking. Of course I didn't ask him directly, but we got to talking. And the beautiful women who aren't young any more have to work at it all the harder. We see that all the time with Madame's clients. Some of them come into the New York salon two and three times a week and spend hours there. They feel safer shut away, being pampered and flattered."

"That sounds like a good lead. I'll have Sergeant Terrizi get on to the hairdressers right away."

She looked so girlishly pleased that he was glad he'd equivocated. "Tell me, who do you think killed Madame Velanie?"

"I'd like to say Jason. But I think my feelings about him may have prejudiced me too much. Because it really doesn't seem like the way he is. Not that kind of killing. Celia Grant told me about seeing the—the body." She struggled to control herself, but one brief sob, more like a gasp for air, broke through.

McDougal got up and went around the desk and put a

hand on her shoulder. "You've been remarkably helpful. And it means all the more because you were closer to her than anyone else."

Tremulous smile.

"And now I want you to go to the infirmary and have the nurse give you a sedative."

That roused her. "I couldn't, with so much to do. I must call Madame's salons—Paris, London, Rome, all the others—so they'll hear it first from me."

He realized work would be more of a tranquilizer for her now than any pill.

"And I'd like you to call the lawyer who handled her will."

She nodded, already ticking off chores in her head.

"Has she any family still living?"

"Her only sister died two years ago. That was the last time Madame changed her will that I know of. But she sensed I didn't like Jason and she could be very cunning— I mean secretive—sometimes. Even with me. So I'll check with the other lawyers she used, just in case there's a later will." She stood up. "I have all the phone numbers in my office."

McDougal thought of suggesting she wait awhile to go back to the office so close to Velanie's. He wished he could be sure the body had been removed.

"I'm all right now. And Mrs. Vining will be in the office right next door to mine. She'll already have started calling the media."

The last word amused him and made him think she'd be all right. He walked with her to the door.

"What do you think of Mrs. Vining?"

"The best publicity woman we ever had. And such a nice, brave person. With all her worries—her husband's illness, I mean—she's gone right on doing a fine job. I'm so glad Madame gave her that money. She deserved it."

"Did you see her this morning?"

"Early, around eight-thirty. And she left a note on my desk while I was in with Madame. It was with the sketch Mrs. Ramsdale did. That was the one nice thing that happened today. I already told Mrs. Ramsdale. I took the sketch in to Madame before I went to the Oaks and she was thrilled. She was like a child in some ways. Having a tantrum one minute, and excited and happy the next."

"I'm glad Velanie saw the sketch." It occurred to him he hadn't seen it himself. Lucy would expect him to comment on it; she could be like a child herself, eating up praise as greedily as candy. "Do you know what Velanie did with it?"

"When I left, she had it propped on her desk in front of a photograph of herself." A sad little smile. "She used to drive photographers crazy, telling them to make her look twenty or thirty years younger. But she was still very handsome. You'd never have guessed she was almost seventy."

McDougal wasn't interested in Velanie's age, not at the moment. "The sketch isn't on the desk now. Do you have any idea what she'd have done with it?"

"Mrs. Vining would probably know. She may have taken it back herself, to send to a magazine."

"I'll walk back with you and ask her."

He had a sudden unreasoning hunch the drawing wouldn't turn up. He hoped Lucy wouldn't be upset; she was more apt to be bloody mad. But once she'd blown off steam, she'd calm down and help him figure out why.

For the first time on the case, he felt he might be on the track of something. Or, rather, he felt as if he'd grabbed the end of a string that might take him where he wanted to go.

8

WHEN LUCY EMERGED from the little gilded-cage elevator in the basement, she was struck by the contrast to that morning. There were only two young instructors in sight, huddled together by the weighing machine talking in undertones. She thought they were two of the interchangeable, leggy lot who had been with Miss Baskie that morning, and she could guess what they were talking about.

"Where can I find Marta Galt?"

The instructors exchanged worried looks.

"I'm not the murderer," Lucy said. "I'm not even slightly dangerous. And I'm working with Inspector McDougal."

"Are you the lady who was down here this morning making sketches?"

Lucy swung her tote bag in confirmation. She had decided to bring her sketching gear along to allay any nervous fears about what she was up to. "What a good memory you have." Privately, she thought they were stupid not to have recognized her instantly. "If you'll just tell me which room Marta Galt is in right now." And please God she's here.

"She's still in the three-o'clock class for Body and Mind Lift. It will be over in—" the instructor consulted a wall clock—"about ten minutes, if you'd like to wait outside. Next to last door on your right—Exercise Room B."

Lucy sensed that unlike Miss Baskie, who had wanted to take her over and act as guide that morning, these young instructors had every intention of sticking together, either for safety or to finish their gossiping, or both. As she started down the corridor, one of them said, "Miss Grant thought it would be better for the clients if everybody kept to the schedule as usual. It's what Madame—" An avid gleam came into her discreetly mascaraed eyes. "Is it true the murderer cut off her head?"

"Only bashed it with a dumbbell. I found the body," Lucy said, and kept going. As an exit line, it had flair.

Standing by the door of Exercise Room B, she could hear one voice going on and on. It sounded like the voice she'd heard that morning on the tape recorder—Miss Tringle's—and she was hesitant about barging in. Better wait till the class was over and get Marta Galt off alone.

Normally, waiting was a form of passiveness that Lucy found irritating, or even intolerable, but she had plenty to think about.

What had Marta Galt said that morning about having known Jason "all too well in New York before—" Before what? If she and Jason had been lovers until Velanie walked in and dangled her money as bait to lure Jason into marriage, then Marta might well have been in a murderous mood. Or she and Jason might have plotted the killing together, with Marta safely in the dining room to fix her own alibi while Jason did the dirty work. In that case,

129

she'd stay on afterward to keep up the pretense that she'd come to the spa only to be done over. When Marta had eavesdropped on Lucy's conversation on the terrace with the inspector and Terrizi, she must have heard more than she'd bargained for, especially about Jason and Celia.

How was she carrying it off now? Lucy turned the doorknob of Exercise Room B very slowly and quietly, opened the door a crack, and looked in.

An instructor, presumably Miss Tringle in the flesh, a slightly older, more muscular version of the norm, stood with her back to the right-hand wall, which was composed entirely of mirrors. Five women, including Marta Galt, sat cross-legged on the floor facing Miss Tringle and their own perspiring reflections. Each had her arms held rigidly in front of her at chest level, with her two hands interlocked.

"By pitting one muscle against the other," Miss Tringle was saying, "you revitalize the pectorals and firm the breasts while you fight that upper-arm flabbiness. Now, while you hold that position . . ."

Marta seemed to be listening with total absorption, her body tense with effort. Whether she was a murder accomplice or a newscaster on the track of a big story, it seemed to Lucy incredible that an intelligent woman could occupy herself seriously with this trivia just hours after the killing. She was basking in her own superiority when something Miss Tringle said yanked at her attention: ". . . and to firm the jaw muscles and prevent or banish a double chin, jut your chin forward, thrust out the lower lip and swivel the head slowly, first left, then right, fifty times. . . ."

Lucy jutted her chin, stuck out her lower lip, swiveled her head like a metronome, and decided that her own exercise, the one she'd done every day for years—simply

130

sticking out her tongue as far as it would go for a count of one hundred—was much simpler and better.

"But in order to get the full benefit of the exercise, you must think happy thoughts. It only takes thirteen facial muscles to give your face the *up* look of happiness. But it takes all fifty-five facial muscles to look sad or out of sorts."

As the ladies pitted their arm muscles, jutted their chins, swiveled their heads, and breathed heavily, the overall effect was not so much of happy thoughts as of imminent apoplexy.

"All right, girls, at ease."

Only Marta Galt gave the impression of being genuinely at ease now, yawning and stretching like a cat. The four other women had a concerted air of tensing for the next round.

". . . And for the last few minutes of class, I want to talk about Mind Lift and the effect it can have on your relationship with others. You all remember Scheherazade, the beautiful captive who was sentenced to be killed, but to gain time she asked to entertain the sultan, her captor, with stories. And she did that so charmingly, night after night, that she won not only her freedom but his heart. Nobody remembers the name of that king—actually, it was Schariar—but that clever girl Scheherazade is immortal. It wasn't her beauty that saved her, although of course that helped. But it was her delightful conversation that really did the trick."

The woman with the blue rinse and crêpey throat, whom Lucy remembered from the Yoga class that morning, said, "If I tried to talk all night, my husband would ram a pillow down my throat."

The instructor looked pained. "Of course we must know when to stop. And meditation is important, too. But instead of transcendental meditation, I suggest Occidental meditation as more suited to our modern American ideal of A Whole Woman. So instead of repeating a mantra over and over, as the transcendentalists do, why not a chantra or en-chantra, of five magic words: 'Beauty of Body and Mind.' "

Lucy looked at her watch: three-twenty-seven. She saw Marta Galt uncross her legs and thought, Ready, get set.

". . . A self-actualized woman—actualized in mind and body—is the ideal we must aim for today. And I must tell you that all of us here at the spa are proud of the way you've carried on with pursuing that goal in spite of the—er—misfortune—that befell Madame Velanie today. Mrs. Meecham is the only one of you who chickened out and asked permission to go home."

Blue-rinse waved her hand frenziedly in the air. "Mrs. Meecham has very high blood pressure, and she's not supposed to have any excitement."

Miss Tringle shrugged. "We all have our little weak spots. The thing is not to give in to our Achilles' heel in a pinch. By the way, you'll be glad to hear no reporters will be allowed to interview you about the death of Madame."

The "girls" looked decidedly unglad. "Our public-relations expert, Mrs. Vining, will take care of that end of things. But if any of the media manage to waylay you, call the switchboard to report it and he or she will be ejected at once."

Several of the ladies looked at Marta Galt, either accusingly or hopefully. Lucy thought it was the latter. Miss Tringle had noticed it, too.

"Mrs. Galt is here in her private capacity. I'm sure she realizes that."

Marta Galt smiled seraphically.

132

"Now, girls, don't forget your four-o'clock mineral oil. On the first week of this diet regime, you are eating your own fat like bacon, and the results will thrill you more than any gourmet goodies. Happy losing—see you tomorrow."

Marta Galt was first out the door and didn't seem at all surprised to see Lucy. "Let's get out of here fast." But at the elevator, she hesitated. "We're supposed to use the stairs for exercise."

"For God's sake, stop acting like a schoolgirl and get in."

As soon as they were in the elevator, Lucy attacked. "You had no right to hang out your window and listen to a private conversation. If you try to use any of that on your program, you'll be in serious trouble—if you aren't already." She wasn't quite sure what she meant by the "if you aren't already" but she hoped it would make Marta nervous.

It didn't. "You sound like my boss. He's scared stiff of libel. I phoned him about Velanie and all he'll use are a few straight facts on the six-thirty news." She shrugged. "No skin off my ass. I'm on vacation."

It sounded incredibly offhand. As the elevator door opened on the ground floor, Lucy said, "I want to ask you some questions. We can use my room."

Marta was already pressing the button for Two. "Come on up with me. I have to take my gourmet goodie at four."

The lettering on the door of Marta's room said "Number 11—RED DEVIL." Below this was a nameplate with a hand-lettered card inserted: "Mrs. Galt."

Marta opened the door, waved her visitor to a chair near the dressing table, and said, "I'd better take it now before I forget." She disappeared into the bathroom, and Lucy

133

thought rather dizzily, Would Lady Macbeth have remembered to take her mineral oil? It seemed unlikely.

She noticed a leather-framed snapshot on the dressing table, of a man in tennis whites holding a racket and looking beamish. His hair was almost as short as McDougal's, his mouth was too wide, his legs were bandied, and, against all odds, he was attractive.

As soon as Marta came out and sat down, Lucy pointed to the snapshot. "He looks like a darling."

Like the Before and After photographs on TV commercials, Marta's face underwent an extraordinary transformation: she looked ten years younger, verging on dewy. "He's the reason I'm here. It's to be a surprise for him when he gets back from London." She slapped her thighs. "Eleven pounds off already, and I'll lose eight more by the time I leave."

So where did Jason come in? Lucy, who was trying to think how to word her next question, said absently, "What a nice surprise for a husband."

"Husband!" Marta's face underwent another transformation, this time to bared-teeth fury. "The only way I'll surprise that bastard is to get a divorce settlement that will clean him out. Know what he did? He asked for a divorce so he could marry his secretary. Said I only thought of my career but she only thought of *him*. The stinker told everybody in town before he told me. Of all the humiliating tricks. That's why I latched on to Jason. I met him at a party, and when he made a pass, I practically fell on my knees. I could hardly wait to go to bed with him. And I wanted to show him off all over town." She laughed harshly. "Some ego builder he is."

Jason the Golden Fleece, Lucy thought.

"We'd be sitting in a restaurant, and whenever another

woman went by our table, Jason's eyes would pop out of his head and roll down the other dame's knockers. So after a few months of that, little Marta retired from the scramble of who fucks who. I was going to 'live for my work.' " Her face softened, and she picked up the framed snapshot. "Until I met him. You'd like him." Lucy was ready to love him. In a rush of good feeling, she said, "I'll try to give you first crack at the story when we find out who murdered Velanie."

"Got any leads yet?"

It was so matter-of-fact, so devoid of gratitude, that Lucy rather regretted her promise. "You'd like us to hang it on Jason."

Marta scowled, considering. Finally she said, "He has the morals of a tomcat but he's lazy. If Velanie threw him out, it would be more like him to go off and find another cushy berth."

"What if she threatened to smear his reputation so he'd never get another job in a gym?"

Marta's laugh was more a hoot. "She'd have to smash his beautiful face and break his legs to do him any real harm in that business. They don't choose male instructors for their good-conduct rating. Knowing Jason, I'd guess he already has something going here, with one of those leggy dolls. Or maybe a side dish tucked away in Wingate."

Lucy decided not to mention Celia Grant. And she certainly wasn't going to mention the inspector's ex-wife. As soon as Hilda Simms had mentioned Mrs. Torrance, the name had rung a loud, clear bell in Lucy's mind: a set designer had once told her the name of the director Eileen ex-McDougal had married. And the look on McDougal's face, when Hilda Simms mentioned trying to track down Mrs. Torrance, had been confirmation enough. She'd realized instantly why he'd phoned her the night before from New York. He'd heard from somebody, probably Terrizi, that his ex-wife was in Wingate, and he'd wanted to be sure she wasn't bothering Lucy. In retrospect, this made his phone call even more gratifying to Lucy. And if Eileen was somehow linked to Jason, it was none of Marta Galt's business.

"We'd need something more solid than that. Did you see anybody acting oddly today? Perhaps around lunchtime?"

"Acting odd is the norm around here. Especially when they're ready to feed the animals. The minute the lunch bell sounds, we race to the dining room like a pack of starving wolves. Know what we had this noon? Endive-and-chicory salad with a dressing that tasted like mineral oil." She looked at the snapshot tenderly. "When he gets home, I'll leave teeth marks all over his sweet skinny body."

Lucy gave up. She was at the door when Marta said, "Wait a minute! I just remembered. Right after we started lunch, I saw that scruffy ex-husband of Velanie's go down the hall toward her office. About twelve-thirty. Ask him where he went."

The young cop stationed outside Velanie's office hailed McDougal with such relief that his neatly trimmed whiskers quivered. "Boy, Inspector, am I glad to see you!" Belatedly, he remembered his manners. "Officer Willoughby, sir, state police. Barracks C, Danbury." Then he rushed on, "Five different ladies have been here nagging me. They said they just wanted to take a peek inside. One asked me if there were bloodstains. She said she'd never seen bloodstains from a murder before."

"You should have told her it looks better on color TV. We'll lock up the place right now."

McDougal took out the key he'd borrowed from Hilda Simms, but before inserting it into the lock, he went back in to make a quick search for Lucy's sketch. After he'd looked in the desk drawers, on the off chance Terrizi had somehow missed it there, he flipped up the edges of the rug while the young cop watched.

"If you'd tell me what you're looking for, sir—"

McDougal told him, and described the approximate size. The youngster went immediately to the desk and lifted the big blotter. "My mother always stashes—" His eager look evaporated as he saw the empty surface. But then he bent closer to look, and suddenly lifted the blotter by the edges to examine the underside.

"Looks like dried blood." He was so excited his voice cracked like a boy soprano's. "Just a trace on the desk, as if it had seeped through, but here on the blotter—look."

McDougal was already beside him, looking. "Either blood or red ink." But red ink wouldn't have left that trace of dried residue. And if it was blood, it had to be Velanie's. Somebody had come in through Hilda Simms's office while it was empty, while Willoughby was outside the door coping with ghouls who wanted to see bloodstains, and retrieved the sketch that had been hidden under the blotter. But why put it there in the first place?

"Let's move the desk over against that side door right now, before we lock up."

He was disgusted with himself for not making a real search earlier, but he didn't want to take it out on the boy. "Good work. I think you may have something here. Scrape off a sample from the wood, put it in an envelope—you'll find some in the middle drawer—and send it

137

right off to the lab with the section of blotter. Mark the envelope, 'Scraping of what may be blood from desk top—compare with victim's.' And sign it, 'Officer Willoughby, assisting in murder investigation.' "

He felt slightly better when he saw the youngster's rapt face.

When he left Willoughby, he stopped outside the next office, where he'd left Hilda Simms, and picked up the key to Velanie's office. Should he tell her now about the missing sketch? Better wait till the lab had analyzed the stains. She'd been through enough.

He took out his frustration by pushing the bell of the next office, PUBLICITY, so hard it sounded like an angry bee.

"Come in. I'm on the phone."

The woman sitting at the desk waved him gracefully to a chair opposite her and went on talking: "I'll let you know later about the memorial service. But you can release what I've given you right away. And you might want to mention that Velanie had already picked her successor, Celia Grant. She's doing a fabulous job here as director at the spa, and she'll inherit the biggest share of the stock. . . . Not at all, sweetie. I'll call you for lunch."

When she hung up, McDougal said, "Mrs. Vining?"

"I think so." She laughed shakily. "It's been such a nightmare day I'm not sure who I am."

He was disarmed by her naturalness. She looked exhausted, but even with dark smudges under her eyes, the eyes themselves were bright with intelligence and they were looking at him very directly. "Have you seen Lucy? How is she? She was so incredibly brave today when we—" She shivered. "Sorry. I'm still rather off balance. And I've been on the phone nonstop: wire services, net-

138

works, the *Times*." She rubbed the back of her neck wearily. "Velanie adored making news, and I'm determined to get her every bit of space going. She was incredibly good to me. And even more since my husband's been ill."

The inspector said Lucy had told him about Mrs. Vining's husband. "I'm sorry. It must have been hard to do the job with that on your mind."

"It's been hell. But I was trained in the old school, like Lucy. We work like mules no matter what hits us."

McDougal wondered how Lucy would like being compared to a mule.

"I understand you're taking your husband to Zurich for treatment."

"As soon as possible. You heard about Velanie giving me the money?"

The inspector nodded. "Was she always that open-handed?"

"God, no. She could be Scrooge and Hetty Green combined. And totally single-minded when it came to business. If she got a new idea, she'd phone you at any hour of the night to discuss it. She was like a kettle that has to toot when it comes to a boil."

"Was she tooting this morning when you saw her?"

"Bubbling. She was excited about a sketch Lucy had made, and it had given her all kinds of ideas. She was ordering new exercise suits, and she wanted a publicity brochure with a half-dozen of the sketches—"

"I'm afraid the first sketch can't be featured. It seems to have disappeared."

Adele Vining dropped her hands on the desk. "Oh, no! Maybe Hilda Simms took it. It has to be somewhere around."

"Miss Simms saw it last in Velanie's office."

139

"But who—if it doesn't turn up, Lucy will kill me." She laughed shakily. "That's not a very bright thing to say right now. Forgive me. But you know how Lucy can be when she gets into one of her tempers, and then it's over as fast as a summer storm. I love that woman and I love her work—always have. The sketch *has* to be around here. Why would anybody take it?"

"I was hoping you could tell me."

"It doesn't make sense. Charming as the sketch is, it's not a Picasso, worth a fortune. Why would somebody think it was valuable?"

The inspector said he intended to find out. "Somebody must have gone in through Hilda Simms's office while she was away. Did you hear anything or see anybody?"

"I was in the infirmary for a while. It must have been then."

The inspector said noncommittally, "Could be. And after you got back you were busy on the phone."

He took Adele Vining through a recap of what had happened that noon, and her story was essentially the same as Lucy's. Velanie had called her again just before twelve-thirty, wanting to see them both right away. "Velanie said she'd already called Lucy, and I've told you what she was like. When she was hot on something, she couldn't wait, and she'd snap out orders like a general. So I went right over to Lucy's room to pick her up."

"Why didn't you just meet her in Velanie's office?"

"Because I know Lucy and I wanted to make sure she'd come. If somebody tells her rat-a-tat-tat 'Do this—do that. Come here. Go there,' she's apt to get stubborn. But you know that better than I do."

The half-amused, half-rueful expression on McDougal's face gave her the answer.

140

"She takes a bit of handling but she's worth it. Whenever you get a totally amenable artist, you've got a hack. I learned that early on in the magazine business."

"Are you ever unreasonable yourself?"

"Of course. That's why I get along so well with artists and writers."

"And with Velanie?"

"I couldn't afford to fight her. I had to hang on because this job means too much to me. As you can see, I'm long past the flitting stage."

She didn't say it as if she were angling for a compliment; she said it tiredly. "With Velanie dead, things may go to pieces anyway but I hope and pray not. Celia would do a good job as head of the business. She's been trained for it."

"But if Velanie had suddenly turned against the girl—say, this morning—and threatened to change her will, mightn't Celia have been desperate enough to kill her?"

"But Velanie hadn't turned against her. Furious at Jason—yes—but not at Celia."

"Did you know Jason and Celia were sleeping together?"

She said sharply, "Who told you that? Lucy? She always did leap to conclusions."

McDougal found it interesting that Adele Vining was so determined to cover for Celia. He deliberately picked up the hint she'd thrown—hurled—at him just before. "You say Velanie was furious at Jason."

Adele Vining nodded. "She'd even sent Hilda Simms into town to check on some carnivorous female staying at the Oaks who'd phoned Jason here."

That was no carnivorous female—that was my ex-wife. He hoped Terrizi had located a hairdresser who'd give Eileen an alibi for the crucial time around noon.

"I will say the messy marriage wasn't all Jason's fault," Adele said. "He thought he'd found the pot of gold in Velanie, and she encouraged that notion till they were married. Then he discovered he'd got a rich old harridan who kept him on a short leash. It must have been galling for him. And if she decided to toss him out, as she threatened to do today— But I mustn't be unfair."

Mustn't you indeed? "Did you know she had some kind of violent argument with Arnold Wynn this morning? Somebody heard her yelling at him."

"Lucy and I both heard her. But I'm used to Velanie, and Lucy isn't. It's odd—half the time I still talk about Velanie as if she were alive." She pushed back a lock of hair. "Wishful thinking. Where was I? Oh, about yelling at Arnold. Velanie almost never said a civil word to that old sot except when they were going over balance sheets. For some reason, she still trusted his judgment on tax problems. And when he's sober, he may be brighter than I think." She shrugged, dismissing Arnold. "Ask Hilda Simms."

The inspector didn't say he already had. "Miss Simms thinks a great deal of you."

"That woman's a saint. Funny, I never thought of saints as super-efficient. I picture them as well-meaning but muddly. But Hilda's the exception. Whenever Velanie was in a rage, Hilda would walk right into the firing line and calm things down."

"I understand she worked for both of you."

"Theoretically. But Velanie took up most of her time. Mostly I—" there was a second's hesitation—"I typed my own stuff when we were up here. But now that Celia will be the head of the business, I hope she'll keep the secretary she has and let me have Hilda full time."

"Wouldn't Celia be the logical person to have first claim on a paragon?"

"They don't get along too well together."

And you know why but you aren't about to tell me. "You've been very helpful." The cliché had a double edge. He thought Adele Vining had been more helpful than she knew.

He had planned to interview Jason next, but now he decided to concentrate first on Celia Grant.

As it turned out, Jason wasn't around anyway.

9

THE OLD PUBLIC-SCHOOL TIE in Wingate, Connecticut, differs considerably from that of, say, Eton. For one thing, there is none of the British double talk, saying "public school" when one means private and expensive. And in Wingate, the old school tie is nothing to wear around the neck; it is simply a bond among classmates, elastic enough to stretch. Sergeant Terrizi, in tracking down Inspector McDougal's ex-wife, was lucky enough to hit on two public-school acquaintances, the first extending back to third grade.

This was a jouncy-busted, blond, bewigged operator at the second hairdresser's shop he tried. She was shampooing a customer whom she deserted instantly, at the soapy Medusa stage, when she saw her old school friend come in.

And within two minutes she was consulting the appointment book.

"Yeah, I thought so but I hadda check the name. Mrs. Torrance. She was my Shampoo, Set for eleven this morning. I gave her a color rinse—Siberian Sable—and

144

shaped the back, and Molly gave her a manicure. So she didn't leave here till about one. I remember she'd just paid when Molly got a call from her kid sister who works at the spa. The kid tells Molly about Madame Velanie being murdered, and of course Molly's so excited she screams it out to the rest of us. I'd got out Mrs. What's-her-name— Torrance's—change from a twenty—ten dollars and some silver. But after she heard about Madame, would you believe it, that dame says 'Keep it,' and tears out, jumps into her car, and takes off. I know it was her car—bright red— because I told her as soon as she came in that was a no-parking zone and she'd better move the car or get a ticket, but she just shrugs."

It was the sort of high-handed disregard of the law Terrizi would have expected of McDougal's ex-wife, but he had to ignore it to concentrate on the larger issue. "You're sure she was here all the time from eleven to one?"

"Are you kidding? Of course I'm sure. Whaddya think—she left a dummy sitting under the hair-dryer and sneaked out? Ask Molly if you don't believe me. Molly did her nails while she dried."

It seemed solid enough. "You happen to know where she went when she left here?"

"All I know is, she's staying at the Oaks. Whyn't you go ask there? Tony Manetta's on the desk all day—just started last week."

Tony was not only part of the old-school-tie network, but also a bowling buddy, and he greeted Terrizi jovially. "You come to rent a room to bring some broad to? I'll tell Angie she shoulda got engaged to me instead of you."

"She should sink so low. Listen, I need your help. You got a Mrs. Torrance staying here—" He started to describe the ex-Mrs. McDougal but Tony guffawed. "You think

I'm senile or something. I remember a good-looking dame inch by inch. But you're too late. She checked out an hour ago."

This was good news, up to a point, but the sergeant wanted to make sure no loose ends of the lady were left dangling. "Did she leave a forwarding address?"

"The Plaza, New York."

Terrizi would have preferred the forwarding address to be Outer Mongolia. But at least she'd left Wingate. "O.K. Thanks. I owe you one."

"Forget it. Just loan me Angie for an evening and we're square."

Terrizi made a derisive noise.

"That's a very ungenerous attitude. I was gonna tell you something else, but two can play stingy."

Terrizi didn't go so far as to trade in Angie for more information, but he did offer to set up a bowling evening soon, to include her. "But you bring your own date."

"Whyn't we just make it a threesome? Then if you get called back for duty on another killing or something . . ." Tony smoothed his brilliantined hair and tweaked his neat mustache, indicating *Roué moves in*.

"Have you got more information for me or haven't you? I have to get back to the spa. Inspector McDougal's already there on the case."

Tony Manetta slapped his low forehead. "Have I got information! I clean forgot to tell you about the letter Mrs. Torrance left here to be mailed. Guess who it's to."

"Inspector McDougal." Terrizi sounded fatalistic. He had all too clear a recollection of the last time Mrs. Torrance had written her ex-husband.

"How come you knew? You a mind reader or something?"

146

"Did you already mail it?"

Tony indicated the open cardboard box marked "Outgoing Mail" on the counter. "Mail isn't picked up till five."

"Then why don't I take it along with me and give it to him, to save time?"

"That's tampering with the U.S. mails."

"It isn't in the U.S. mail yet. And the inspector would get it a day sooner. I can deliver it to him within a half hour."

"You're not pulling a fast one on me?"

Terrizi swore he was not. With the letter safely in his jacket pocket, he was about to beat a quick retreat when his friend said, "Some cop you are—not even asking me what else I got to tell you. Know who tore in here wanting Mrs. Torrance twenty minutes after she pulled out?" He rocked back on his elevator heels, smirking.

"Who?"

"The dead dame's husband. That's who. He came about three o'clock."

The sergeant howled a four-letter word. While he'd been sitting on Lucy Ramsdale's terrace at the spa, the prime suspect had taken off. "That bastard. I let him go clean himself up and recover from shock, but I warned him not to leave the premises. So I turn my back and he gets away."

"He didn't get far. He's in the taproom right now."

Terrizi whirled and took off, setting what was perhaps a new world record for the twenty-yard dash.

His quarry was the only customer in the taproom. He was sitting in the far corner, with a musket on the wall behind hanging heavily over his head. The Oaks Inn, which went back to Revolutionary days when Benedict Arnold fought the British in Wingate and had his horse shot out from under him, had been redecorated in a big way for the Bicentennial. Afterward, the Inn had held on to the quaint touches such as muskets and warming pans, because they'd proved especially popular with tourists.

Ye olde quaintness and, even more, the stiff prices for drinks had made it a less than popular hangout for Sergeant Terrizi's generation. They preferred the Hungry Bear, which served beer and the best hamburgers in town for considerably less strain on the wallet.

Normally, Sergeant Terrizi would have felt out of place here, but not now; he strode over to the corner. "What the hell do you think you're doing?"

Jason looked up and said simply, "Drinking."

Terrizi couldn't help noting that although Jason was probably stoned, he didn't have the dull-eyed look of a drunk. And he didn't look haggard; he looked as if he were suffering, but it didn't spoil his incredible good looks.

Jason had tilted up his nearly empty glass and drained it. "While you're up, would you mind getting me another Jack Daniels and water? Charge it to Velanie's account. The bartender knows me."

Terrizi banged down the glass Jason had handed him and sat down himself so he could lower his voice. "I know you came here looking for Mrs. Torrance. What did you want with her?"

"I wanted to ask her a favor. But she'd left town."

"Lucky for you. She's the ex-wife of Inspector McDougal, who's in charge of this murder case."

Jason considered this. "Funny, she didn't act like an inspector's wife."

"Did you want her to give you an alibi so you wouldn't be charged with murder?"

"Shouldn't you advise me of my rights before you say things like that?"

A red-faced Terrizi mumbled the usual warning. ". . . remain silent. And you have the right to consult a lawyer."

"The only lawyers I know are Velanie's. And they'd think I killed her."

Terrizi refrained from saying, So do I. "Where were you between the hours of twelve and one today?"

"I can't tell you. I'm a gentleman." He pronounced gentleman slowly and carefully, but rather spoiled the effect by adding, "Sometimes."

The sergeant began to feel protective in spite of himself. "You ought to get a lawyer right away."

"Could you recommend one who didn't cost too much? Velanie left me some money but I won't get it for a while. She was going to change her will, you know, and cut me out. She told me so this morning."

Terrizi had never had a suspect behave so perversely. "Listen. You're coming with me right now. I'll take you to the inspector."

"I'd rather not see him until I've worked out a good alibi."

"Innocent men don't need alibis when their wives get murdered." Even to Terrizi, it sounded stuffy; he felt he should have stated it differently.

Jason wagged a finger at his companion. "I can tell you're not a married man."

Terrizi bristled. "I soon will be. To the best-looking girl in Wingate."

"Don't let her come near me. I'm fatal to women."

"She wouldn't give you the time of day. Or night either."

"Wanna bet?"

The bartender brought over two large cups of black coffee. "Compliments of the house."

"Thanks."

149

"I'd rather have a drink," Jason said plaintively. The bartender understood from Sergeant Terrizi's expression that this was not a feasible idea. When the man had gone, Terrizi said, "Now, come on, drink that coffee. You want to sober up before you see the inspector."

"I—do—not—want—to—sober—up. When I'm sober, I remember the way she looked with her brains spilled out and—" Jason suddenly looked green. He put his hand to his mouth, making "hic" sounds that signaled trouble.

"Not again!" Terrizi said.

As Jason bolted for the men's room in the hall, the sergeant, looking pained, followed.

Officer Willoughby stood at attention in front of the inspector's borrowed desk. "I tracked down Miss Grant, sir. Her secretary said Miss Grant was in conference and couldn't be disturbed, but we got on more friendly terms because she has a sister living in Hartford so that established a bond."

McDougal looked at the beaming youngster and was divided between amusement and impatience. "So what did the secretary whisper in your ear after you'd established a bond?"

"Miss Grant is on the lower floor—I mean, like the basement—having a facial. She didn't want the police to know, because she thought it might seem disrespectful to the dead. But the secretary said Miss Grant felt it was what Madame Velanie would have wanted—to keep up appearances for the sake of the clients' morale."

"That's one way to explain it."

"I thought I'd better check with you to see if you want me to go down there and fetch her right now. She'll be through at four-thirty. But if I barge in and pull her out

now, she might stiffen up and be somewhat uncoopera-
tive. If we let her finish, sir—ladies are more apt to be
relaxed after a facial."

As an expert on ladies who had facials, Willoughby was
about as likely as a newborn calf. But as a newly minted
cop using his head, he was doing rather well.

"I think you're right, Officer. We'll take her in a relaxed
state at four-thirty. But don't let her get away. Nab her as
soon as she gets off the elevator and hustle her right along
to me. In a chivalrous way, of course."

"Of course, sir. But she won't be coming up on the elevator. The secretary said Miss Grant always walks up the
stairs because it's considered better for the figure. Madame
Velanie insisted on that for the clients, and the staff has to
set an example. So the secretary showed me where the
stairs are, and if it's all right with you, sir, I'll station
myself there now. Miss Grant might be through a few
minutes early."

The inspector thought that Willoughby, in the space of
ten or so minutes, had cemented quite a relationship with
the secretary. He said solemnly, "An excellent idea, Officer."

"There's a basement exit to the outside, but I can keep it
in view from the stairwell."

"Fine. I'll expect you in ten or fifteen minutes."

When the knock came at the door soon after Willoughby had gone, McDougal said in a mild tone, "Come
in," and was half out of his chair to greet the lady when
somebody definitely not a lady came in.

"You remember me, sir? Detective Carlin, homicide,
state police."

"I certainly do, Carlin." Even if I'd forgotten your
name, I'd remember your face forever.

Detective Carlin was pudgy and walked with a slight waddle, but his memorable features were the eyes so ringed with black shadows that they gave him a strong resemblance to a raccoon. "I brought two troopers with me. Inspector Hanson thought you might need 'em."

"Good. We'll need at least two on guard duty here tonight. The first thing I'd like you to do is interview the cleaning women. Find out when they collect trash—I mean, empty the wastebaskets. If they've left for the day, check with the housekeeper and she'll know how to reach them. We're looking for a sketch that's disappeared. Ask them if they happened to notice scraps of a torn-up watercolor sketch. It was done by an artist here this morning, and was last seen in one piece in Madame Velanie's office soon before she was killed." He told Carlin briefly about the possibility that blood had splashed on the sketch. "Mrs. Ramsdale doesn't know yet it's missing."

"Mrs. Ramsdale!" Detective Carlin shone with pleasure. "Isn't she the little lady who found the body in the clothes bin? She find this body, too?"

The inspector had to admit it was so.

Carlin said in a doting voice, "Finding bodies is as common to her as fleas to a dog."

It hardly seemed an adequate description of Lucy. "She does other things, too. She's a very good artist."

"She'll be mad as hell if her sketch doesn't turn up in one piece." Carlin's face crinkled in thought. "If it does, maybe we could take off a spot of blood with ink eradicator."

McDougal thought the sketch was probably in an incinerator by now, but Carlin was so pleased with his idea that the inspector only said, "See what you can find out."

The detective was just going out the door when Officer

Willoughby arrived. "Miss Celia Grant to see you, sir."
He might have been a herald blowing a trumpet to usher
in royalty.

McDougal thought, Willoughby likes candy-box covers.
He understood even more when Celia Grant came in.
Even in the simple black dress, her figure was something
to make the birds sing.

Detective Carlin didn't so much exit as back out, his
eyes popping nearly out of his head.

When Celia Grant took the chair facing McDougal, he
was glad the desk cut off his view of her legs.

Officer Willoughby said, "Would you like me to stay,
sir, to take shorthand notes?"

"Thank you, Officer. That won't be necessary."

"I could come back when you're through with Miss
Grant and escort her to her quarters. She's had a horrible
shock, sir. Madame Velanie had been like a mother to
her."

The inspector said untruthfully he'd try not to upset her.
"I'll send for you, Officer, if we need you."

As soon as they were alone, Celia Grant said, "It must
seem heartless of me, Inspector, to be getting a facial at
such a sad time, but we have to set an example for the
clients. And my eyes were so swollen and red from crying."

"Crying about Madame?"

"Of course."

"But you were already red-eyed this morning when you
came to the pool to collect Jason and take him away from
his class."

One quiver of her false eyelashes was the only indica-
tion she gave that he'd startled her. "It was silly of me. But
Madame was in a terrible humor and she was apt to take

out her temper on people close to her. We were terribly close—she and I."

"Do you know what put her in a bad mood?"

"I think Arnold Wynn—that's her ex-husband—had been yammering at her for money."

"Or trying to convince her that you and Jason were sleeping together."

The girl's head jerked back as if she'd been punched in the chin, but after that first involuntary reflex, she sat up very straight and projected outraged innocence. "Inspector, how can you say such a fantastic thing? He was Madame's *husband*."

"I said it because he himself told somebody so last night."

McDougal had meant to startle her, and he thought he'd succeeded, but even that didn't throw her off.

"What a dreadful, ridiculous lie. I can't understand why Jason would say it. Unless he wanted the rumor to reach Madame and turn her against me. But Madame knew the truth: he was having an affair with a Mrs. Torrance, who is staying at the Oaks Inn. Madame herself told me that this morning, and she sent Hilda Simms in to check up on the woman. Didn't Hilda tell you?"

"I happen to know Jason only met Mrs. Torrance yesterday. I believe they had a drink together in a bar. That's hardly what I'd call an affair."

"They must have been meeting before that in New York."

"Let it go," McDougal said harshly. You're handling this badly, he told himself. You're lucky Officer Willoughby isn't here to see you make a mess of things; he'd have done better himself. The idea of Officer Willoughby interviewing Miss Grant made the inspector grin.

"Sorry if I yelled at you. The fact is, we're checking on Mrs. Torrance now. Of course, we're checking on everybody as a matter of routine. I understand from the chef that the kitchen staff is accounted for between the hours of twelve and one. And the—uh—guests were all at lunch. You told Sergeant Terrizi that two instructors are in the main dining room at each meal."

Celia Grant was instantly businesslike, even pedantic. "That is correct. We call it hostessing. And the dietitian and I take a turn, but as you know, she's away this week. And when Madame is in residence here, she has dinner with the guests the opening night of their stay. We call it opening night because in many ways it's the opening of a new life for the clients. . . ."

And what do you call their final evening? The last supper? Aloud, all he said was "Thank you. That makes it very clear. I wish all the people I interview were as concise as you." He was afraid he'd laid it on too thickly, because she didn't say anything for a moment. Then she smiled in a different way, so that her face looked softer and sweeter. "Madame used to tell me, 'Talk in a straight line. Don't give me the adjectives. Save those for the customers.' "

"You must have been a remarkably good student. Mrs. Vining says you'd do a fine job of running the business now."

"Did she say that?" There was no mistaking the surprise and pleasure. "Coming from Mrs. Vining, that's a real compliment. She's so marvelous at her own job. The editors fall all over themselves to use whatever she gives them."

"Would you keep her on until you sell the business?"

"I have no intention of selling the business."

You see yourself as Madame Celia, head of the famous

firm. He decided to throw in some artificial bait. "In an earlier will of Velanie's, you inherit a controlling share of the stock."

She jerked to attention. "What do you mean—an earlier will? Madame made a will last year that still stands."

"Are you sure?"

"Madame would have told me if she'd made any changes."

"Just for the record, where were you between the hours of twelve and one this noon?"

"In my cottage having lunch. I already told your sergeant that."

"You were alone?"

"Of course."

He was quite sure she was lying, but at the moment there was no point in nudging. "It's been a difficult day for you and I won't keep you any longer."

She had been braced for more questions—awkward questions. Now she reminded him of somebody in a game of tug-of-war: with the rope unexpectedly gone slack, she was thrown off balance. She sat there uncertainly for a moment before her marvelous legs got her moving.

McDougal hoped Officer Willoughby was lurking outside, waiting to "escort Miss Grant to her quarters." He might be getting her at a vulnerable moment. The trouble was that Officer Willoughby was considerably more vulnerable than Miss Celia Grant. But at least Willoughby had been bright enough to look under the desk blotter, McDougal reminded himself. That's more than you did.

Thinking of the bloodstain on the blotter reminded the inspector he'd soon have to tell Lucy her sketch was missing. He looked forward to that the way a mobile-home owner looks forward to a hurricane.

"Oh, my God, you scared me nearly silly." Lucy glared at the visitor who had popped out from behind a curtain. "If you ever do that to me again, I'll butt you in the stomach."

"Sorry." Arnold Wynn wiped his perspiring forehead with the handkerchief from his breast pocket, but this time he didn't refold it and put it back with the point protruding nattily: he rammed it in. "I thought it might be the maid coming in, and I didn't want anyone to know I was here. So I ducked behind the drapes until I could be sure it was you."

Lucy detested the word "drapes" but it wasn't the moment to diddle over semantics. "I'm so sorry about Velanie. It was horrible. Have you seen Inspector Mc-Dougal?"

Arnold Wynn moved his head left and then right very slowly, as if any abrupt movement would make it fall off. "I only saw a sergeant. Mind if I sit down?" He almost fell into the small boudoir chair, which creaked in protest.

Lucy had just left Marta, and had come back to her room to call the inspector on the house phone and tell him to question Wynn about the noon visit. But now she was pleased to have the preliminary crack at Wynn herself. And she was remembering an old saying of her grandmother's: "You catch more flies with honey than vinegar."

In a crooning tone, she said, "You look exhausted. You should have had the nurse give you something."

"She did. And then she told me not to drink anything alcoholic for eight hours." Wynn snorted. "If ever I needed a drink, it was then. So I took a short one, but it hit me hard. I was out like a light for over an hour. You found the body, didn't you? What time was that?"

"About twelve-thirty." She was annoyed at his taking charge as if he were interviewing her. To hell with the honey. She said bluntly, "It must have been just after you saw her."

"I didn't see her then. I meant to but"—long pause—"I changed my mind. I didn't see her after about nine-thirty this morning. We had a session then."

"I heard you. At least, I heard Velanie yelling at you. She sounded mad as hell."

"It didn't really mean anything, her yelling like that." His bloodshot eyes were glazed over, and he stared across the room, seeing ghosts. "The truth is, I kind of liked to have her get mad and yell. Reminded me of the old days when we'd fight and make up. Last night she started out yelling—thought I was stoned. But when we began going over the figures, she could see I knew what I was talking about. She always listened to me when we got on to a balance sheet."

"Did you tell her to sell the business for the price they offered to pay?"

"She would never have sold. She liked to flirt with the idea, but she wouldn't have gone through with it."

"That isn't what she was yelling about this morning, though, is it?"

"No." He was focusing on Lucy again. "Whenever you told her something she didn't want to believe, she tried to shout you down. But she always took in what you were saying. And later on, she was apt to come around. I think that's why she was killed. Because I told her about Jason and Celia. And when she thought it over she'd realize I wouldn't lie about a thing like that. In a funny way, she trusted me. So she was done in."

"You mean Jason or Celia or both of them killed her? What makes you think so? Did you see either of them near her office this noon? Or hear their voices when you went by?"

"Just Velanie's. She was talking to somebody."

"In her office?"

He seemed not to hear her, but Lucy had a feeling that now he was sifting, deciding what to tell and what to hold back. She didn't dare hammer at him, for fear he might clam up altogether. She said quietly, "If you could hear what Velanie was saying, you must have an idea of who she was talking to."

This time, he definitely avoided looking at her. "I'll have to think about it."

"Arnold, she was murdered. Don't try to protect her killer."

"I'm not protecting a killer. I already told you, Jason had plenty of motive. And all the more if Velanie tackled him with what I'd told her earlier."

"Then if you think Jason was with her, why not say so? If you don't trust me enough to tell me, tell the inspector. I'll take you to him right now. He's using the dietitian's office."

But she'd gone too fast. As she reached for the phone, Wynn shrank back and clutched the arm of the chair. "Later. I'm still a wreck. When you've been married to a person for twenty years, and then you see her all bloody—" He covered his face with one hand, but he still hung on to the chair arm with the other. "I'll never forget that sight." His sobs sounded genuine, and a few tears dampened his red-veined cheeks, but Lucy thought they might be the easy tears of a boozer. His grief wasn't as wholehearted as he wanted her to think.

She was even more suspicious when he said, "Just to get my mind straight, tell me how you happened to go to Velanie's office and find the body."

"Find the body" was an odd phrase for a grieving husband, even a grieving ex-husband, but Lucy decided to

159

humor him. Something was puzzling him, or worrying him, and if she helped straighten that out, he'd be more willing to talk to McDougal.

"Velanie called me around twelve-thirty. She was crazy about the sketch I'd done this morning, and she wanted me to come see her right away." Lucy went through the whole sequence, up to the moment she'd seen the dead woman, and there was no doubt at all that she had his total attention. For a man who preferred the sound of his own voice, probably next to the gurgle of liquor being poured, he was astonishingly concentrated on every word she was saying.

He only asked one question. "And you're sure Velanie said on the phone, 'Come right away'?"

Lucy said she was positive. "And I know it was her voice. She sounded a bit far away, but that must have been because of the stuff she had on her face. It had hardened like cement." Lucy explained her theory about the timer being reset.

Wynn seemed to be thinking this over; finally he nodded as if he'd solved something to his own satisfaction, but he didn't offer to share it.

Lucy was more than annoyed now; she launched her next remark as if she were firing a howitzer. "We'll see the inspector right now and you'll tell him everything you know. Otherwise, he'll drag it out of you."

It was hardly the most tactful way to snag a reluctant witness.

Wynn leaped up so fast he knocked over the lamp on the bed table, and it was Lucy who caught it before it crashed to the floor.

"I told you—I'm in no condition." He was almost shouting, but then, as if hearing how he sounded, he made an effort to calm down. "I'll try to see the inspector after dinner."

As he turned to go, Lucy saw the flask bulging in his hip pocket. By "after dinner" he might be too drunk to make sense. "Arnold, promise me you won't take another drink before you see McDougal."

Wynn said "I promise" so quickly she suspected it was the glib vow of an alcoholic who wants to avoid a lecture. But he surprised her by adding, "This time I really mean it. I can't afford to get drunk till after I—"

"Till after you what?"

He said evasively, "Till after—after Jason is arrested."

"But if you can prove he did it, then the sooner you say so the better. And the safer you'll be."

"I'll be safe." He sounded almost jaunty.

"That's what they always say in girlish murder mysteries. And then they go out to meet the murderer in the dark of the moon and they end up floating on their face in the lily pond."

Wynn chuckled—not ho-ho-ho, but with real amusement. "I've never been able to float on my face. I can't seem to breathe right."

"That's not any problem—when you're dead."

10

DETECTIVE CARLIN CAME OUT of the maids' locker room in
the basement after drawing a blank all around. The two
cleaning women who were just going off duty had emptied
wastebaskets without seeing a trace of a watercolor sketch,
whole or in pieces. The younger of the two women did say
something about "the things they throw away— Today it
was almost a whole roll of that see-through paper." Detective Carlin, reasonably enough, hadn't followed this up.
And that was a pity, because it was the one bit of evidence
he might have collected. He had been told to ask about a
sketch, and not by any leap of his limited imagination
could he see any connection.

The housekeeper, Mrs. Pollack, had escorted Carlin
down to the basement. "No men are ever allowed down
here except the plumber. And of course the two hairdressers, but they don't really count." She had left him to
find his way back upstairs alone, which he vaguely resented; it was as if she'd decided he was as harmless as the
hairdressers.

162

He was proceeding at his waddling pace down the corridor to the elevator when a hideous scream jabbed his eardrums. "Stop! You're killing me!"

Detective Carlin was of the old school of cop: act before you think. He drew his gun, charged in the direction the voice had come from, and kicked open a door on his right. Steam, thick hot steam, rolled over him, so that at first he couldn't even see. As the mists cleared, he beheld a stout-armed woman in a white uniform advancing on him with a red-hot poker raised in a menacing way. Behind her, a female, mostly naked, was crouched on the floor squealing. "It's a man!" She grabbed a towel from a chair.

"Get out." The uniformed woman glared at the intruder, her red-hot poker still raised. "Men iss *verboten*— forbidden. Put away that gun."

"Wh-what were you doing to her?"

"I cook her." She grinned evilly.

"The lady said you were killing her."

The victim, now wrapped more or less in a towel, laughed. "How sweet. He was going to rescue me. You're a cop, aren't you?"

Detective Carlin drew himself up, although his figure didn't lend itself to this stance, and nodded, he hoped curtly. "Connecticut state homicide."

"You're here about Madame's murder! How marvelous. Do tell me what you've found out."

"We don't discuss a case in progress with outsiders." Detective Carlin did his best to look as if he were privy to sensational developments about which his lips were sealed.

"Then you *have* found something out."

The heat in the room was so overpowering that his face seemed to be melting, but for the first time he was enjoying himself; he felt like a TV detective.

"Was the killer that fabulous-looking husband of Vel-anie's? I could eat him on crackers."

The attendant had gone to the potbellied stove to stir the burning coals. "Enough of diss *Kaffeeklatsch*." She rattled her poker. "Will be like freezing in here. Get out and shut door tight behind you."

"Oh, let him stay a minute. I'm longing to get something juicy to tell the girls."

If she'd been young and beautiful, Detective Carlin might have been reluctant to leave. But she was at least fifty, and lumpy. He said he had to see the inspector and turn in his report. "And as for you"—he pointed at the lumpish female in the towel—"from now on, keep your voice down. When a murder has been committed, a cop is on the alert to prevent more killings. We can't waste time on silly women screaming over nothing." That'll hold her.

It did, too. "Do—do you expect the killer to strike again?"

"They usually do." It was a masterful exit. Banging the door behind him made it even better. He was feeling so on top of things that he was in no great rush to see Inspector McDougal and report that he hadn't found a trace of Lucy's sketch. When he heard voices behind another closed door, he stopped to listen shamelessly.

". . . and fling slices of fresh cucumber into the water."

Bunch of litterbugs, Carlin thought, frowning.

"And as you loll back in your bath, have two more slices on your eyelids, to banish those horrid marks of tiredness."

Detective Carlin grew cucumbers in his backyard in Hartford, and he had eaten them raw and pickled, but he had never put a slice on his eyelids. He wondered if it might fade out the black circles under his eyes.

"And it might interest you to know who installed the

first bathroom. A king, if you please. King Minos of Crete, in 1700, B.C. So we should give three cheers for that king who gave us the royal luxury of a good, long soak to . . ."

There were a few words here the eavesdropper couldn't get; then "perfume in your navel" came out strongly. "And another erotic zone—the nape of the neck. A lover will bury his face there."

Detective Carlin, who had never buried his face in a neck, thought maybe he should try it. The navel bit made him a little nervous.

". . . And for a tingling afterglow when you've dried, rub yourself all over with a friction glove of hemp and horsehair."

Horsehair! Next they'd be using whips. The voice was so soft now he could hardly hear it. "And remember, you may grow loofah in your own little garden."

Like marijuana? Or was loofah a hard drug? Ought to report that to the narcotics boys. Should he mention it to Inspector McDougal first? Might have something to do with the murder.

He had reached the elevator when he noticed the sign: DON'T RIDE! WALK! YOUR FIGURE WILL THANK YOU PRETTILY. He pulled in his stomach and decided to walk.

At the landing, he glanced out the window and saw a man crossing the lawn who looked out of place here. Old guy with a worse paunch than his own, and a funny walk, as if he had the staggers. Wearing his hair flapping down like Benjamin Franklin.

To see somebody at the spa in such seedy condition gave Detective Carlin's ego a lift. He didn't think to mention it to the inspector. Not until much later.

Officer Willoughby had been sent off again to find Arnold Wynn or Jason or both, but hadn't returned.

165

Sergeant Terrizi was still unaccountably missing. And Mc-Dougal's legs were getting stiff from being jammed under the too-low desk in the borrowed office. He untangled himself once more and decided to go see Lucy.

In the past few years, he had developed an instinctive sense of how long she could be left on her own without either getting mad or getting restless enough to do something rash. Rash in *his* judgment, not hers.

Another thing he'd developed since he'd been Lucy's tenant was a real need to talk over a case with her, or as she'd once put it, "Stick in our thumbs and pull out the plums."

The only trouble was that this time he had no ripe plums to offer her as a swap for whatever she'd learned. Somehow he should have got more out of Celia Grant especially, and he could imagine Lucy wearing her look of *Is that all you found out?* But most of all he dreaded the way she'd look when he told her her sketch was missing.

His stride had slowed to a dawdle, and when he got to the door opening onto the main hall, it beckoned like an escape hatch. Ought to go out and get the lay of the land. When he reached the dining room on his left, he glanced in and saw that the two tables were already set for dinner, with rosy-red cloths and crystal. What stopped him cold was the centerpiece on the table nearest the door: a crystal bowl heaped with what looked like hunks of raw broccoli; carrot sticks poked up from this and dark green leaves trailed out onto the cloth. He went closer and saw the leaves were raw spinach.

He was staring at this when he had the uneasy feeling that he, in turn, was being stared at. His glance went to the door at the back of the dining room, presumably leading into the kitchen, and he spotted the peephole at once.

"Inspector!" Chef Ronda emerged, beaming in toothy welcome. "I have the honor to cook dinner for you tonight."

"Eat here?" McDougal's tone had an element of stark horror as he gestured at the tables.

"No, no. Too many radies chirping at once. Rike eating in bird cage at zoo. I serve you in the room of that ruvry rady Mrs. Ramsday. She came to me to ask this favor, and I say to her, 'Is no favor, is privirege.' "

Flowery talk usually affected McDougal like ragweed, but the gist of the chef's message was so pleasant that he said, "How nice of you. I look forward to having some of your dishes."

"Tonight I serve you one of Madame's favorites—diet dish but dericious."

McDougal thought it was an odd twist on funeral baked meats—a non-cholesterol memorial.

"Breakfast and runch, Madame deny hersef. Brack coffee, toast rike dog biscuit. And for runch, fruit, yogurt. But at dinner she eat rike a horse. She ruvved good food, though she often comprain to me about cost, then say, 'Why don't we have robster tomorrow?' She was funny combination of stingy mean and big gesture."

McDougal still had an ingrained distrust of the Japanese acquired in the Navy in World War II. He was surprised to feel none of that with Ronda. On impulse, he said, "If you have a few minutes, I'd like you to tell me your opinion of the others. Miss Grant, for instance."

Chef Ronda drew out a chair for McDougal at the table nearest the front, and sat down opposite him. The inspector tried to keep his eyes off the centerpiece.

"Miss Grant hard worker and very smart rady. Very correct, but I think not by birth. She rearn a part and pray it."

McDougal had to translate this in his head: she learned a part and played it.

"Often code to men."

Code? Secretive?

"Could be rike ice."

Oh, cold.

"But fire under that ice. And if something upset her, bad temper. Not to Madame, or to guests. Onry those she thinks beneath her. She treat me rike short-order cook to start, but I make her understand chef is artist. She has no true enjoyment of food. Chew radyrike bites, caring most about her figure. And even when she eat, brain go tick, tick, tick."

"And the publicity woman, Mrs. Vining?"

Chef Ronda's smile was effulgent. "Charming rady. And I mean rady in true sense. Even if she eats onry five bites at dinner because she is so worried about sick husband, she often come to kitchen to thank me, say how superb. Never forget nice thought for others."

"How about Madame's husband, Jason?"

Ronda shrugged. "Rike a puppy. Eat anything, but most of all, he eat up radies. Can't ever get enough of that dish. Then he go swim or pray tennis to work up more appetite and keep himsef fit. *Un homme très beau*, but not in brain or *honneur*. You watch, he grab off another rich rady soon."

Not if he's indicted for murder, he won't. McDougal got up abruptly. "I'm enormously grateful to you. What time will you serve us dinner?"

"Mrs. Ramsday think seven. She say you have drinks first. She brought her own frask."

McDougal said, "Fine." It would give him almost an hour, and he wanted to see Jason and Wynn.

When he turned into the back corridor, Sergeant Terrizi was just coming toward him. "I thought I might find you in Mrs. Ramsdale's room. I left a note on your desk."

"Come on in. You can tell me instead."

Terrizi's terra-cotta coloring became more cotta. "The note's not from me, sir. It's from your—from Mrs. Torrance. She left it when she checked out this afternoon." Seeing the odd look on McDougal's face, he went on quickly, "She has an airtight alibi for this noon. The hairdresser. I checked that first."

"Good." McDougal's voice sounded remote. He didn't say anything more.

"And when I went to the Oaks afterward, Madame Velanie's husband was in the bar there."

"I've had Officer Willoughby looking for him. Did you bring him back here?"

"Yes, sir." Terrizi drew a gulp of air. "But he passed out on the way. I had to take him over to his cottage and put him to bed. I left one of the state troopers on guard outside the door." He was almost dogtrotting to keep up with McDougal.

In the office, the inspector went right to the desk, and his ex-wife's handwriting on the envelope seemed to leap out and hit him in the face. Read it, he told himself. You'll be no good at concentrating till you've read the damn thing.

"If you'll excuse me for a moment—" He saw the sergeant make a move to leave. "No, stay; won't take a minute."

While the inspector slit the envelope and read, Terrizi, sitting on the edge of a chair, stared at the memo board without seeing anything on it. He was thinking anxiously, If the inspector goes back to that bitch again . . .

"O.K. No problem."

McDougal sounded matter-of-fact. "Eileen heard about

169

the murder while she was still at the hairdresser's and she decided it was better to leave town. Save me embarrassment."

For the first time, the sergeant felt something close to liking for the ex-Mrs. McDougal. "Jason Pappas went to the Oaks this afternoon to see her but she'd already left. I have a hunch he wanted her to give him an alibi, but he was so drunk when I questioned him he wasn't making much sense." Terrizi gave highlights of the conversation with Jason.

"Maybe he was playing drunk so you wouldn't bear down on him."

Terrizi—remembering a scene, with sound effects, in the men's room—said, "I don't think he was acting, sir. But he may be covering up for Celia Grant."

"The iron maiden Celia covers very nicely for herself. She was all haughty innocence when I accused her of having an affair with Jason. She doesn't scare easy. And she's almost certainly lying when she says she was alone in her cottage from twelve to one. A bereaved adopted daughter she is not." He told about Celia Grant having a facial that afternoon.

Sergeant Terrizi didn't share his mother's enthusiasm for wakes, but the idea of anything so nontraditional as a facial shocked him. "Talk about cold-blooded."

Obviously, Terrizi was no longer a champion of the lady. McDougal said, "You think she'd be a more likely killer than Jason?"

"No question about it. He's got a backbone made of putty."

Lucy looked at herself in the long mirror with unabashed pleasure. The creamy-white brocade pants suit fitted perfectly, and she was surprised that the spa had been able to produce a size 10. She had a momentary pitying thought for the paying guests who hadn't her looks or her figure. It didn't occur to her that the instructors like Miss Baskie had something she would never have again—youth. Years before, while her husband was still alive, she had sat in front of the dressing-table mirror in their bedroom and experimented, holding two fingers on each side of her face just in front of the ears, to draw the skin taut. Then she'd turned around and announced to Hal, "I think I'll have my face lifted. Practically everybody's doing it."

"Running faster and faster to stay in one place," he had said. "Come off it. That's like saying you want to wipe out all our years together and start again with a blank. A cipher's unlined, but I'm damned if I want a cipher."

She had never again been tempted to have a face-lift. And she viewed herself now without any of the tremors of a teenager: Do I look all right? Will I know what to say? Will he like me? It didn't occur to her to doubt her own charm, and in this she was probably unique among the occupants of a beauty spa.

McDougal, when he came in, was too tired and frustrated to notice her new finery. He had had Terrizi try to rouse Jason for an interview, but the sergeant reported Jason wouldn't be fit to talk for several hours, if then. All Jason had done was mumble "Lemme alone; I'm sick," and burrow back under the sheet. The trooper stationed outside his door said that once Jason had yelled what sounded like "gave her mother forty whacks." But when the trooper went in to check, Jason seemed to be asleep. The Lizzie Borden doggerel, although it rather pointed to Celia Grant if one substituted an ax for a dumbbell, was hardly what they needed in the way of solid evidence. Nei-

171

ther was Detective Carlin's report that he'd heard an instructor suggest growing loofah secretly at home, "so this might be a case for the narcs." If the inspector had had a wet loofah handy, he might have thrown it in Carlin's plump face. The lab had confirmed that the stains on Velanie's desk blotter and desk were blood, and matched the victim's type, but this in itself didn't point one way or another. Hilda Simms, that paragon of secretaries, was still trying to get any information on Velanie's will out of a junior law partner. The senior partner who had drawn up the will was sailing his boat off Martha's Vineyard, and the Coast Guard would have to locate him. The thought of having to interrupt the senior partner's vacation seemed to upset the junior partner far more than Velanie's murder. Officer Willoughby had been looking for Arnold Wynn without success; the inspector suspected darkly Willoughby had been busier looking at Celia Grant's lower extremities. The boy had reported with barely subdued radiance that he'd been invited to have dinner in the apartment of Miss Grant's secretary in Wingate. "If you don't need me, sir."

In the mood McDougal was in, he came near saying, You're on duty here till ten. But then he thought of a way Willoughby might be really useful on the loose. "I'd like you to pump the secretary very casually over dinner and find out two things."

He told Willoughby the two things, and the young cop went bounding off wagging his tail. It was hard to imagine him pumping a girl casually: he'd probably tip his hand after one glass of domestic sherry.

McDougal had got to Lucy's room about six-thirty. After one look at his drawn face, she forgave him for not noticing her Pierre Cardin pants suit, and made drinks herself. At home, McDougal always made the drinks, so

172

this in itself was quite a gesture. When he said he was getting nowhere fast on the case, Lucy said, "Oh, you always feel that way at first."

After several hefty gulps of Scotch, it seemed to McDougal that she was right. He unknotted his legs on the terrace chaise, put back his head, and began to give her a slightly censored but concise account of his afternoon. All he left out was any mention of her sketch and he was relieved that Lucy didn't ask about it; she was too busy telling him about her session with Marta Galt. "And she did sleep with Jason for a while but she couldn't take his flittering around. Now she's found somebody she wants to marry and she's hell-bent on taking off twenty pounds and firming the flab, so why would she have any reason to kill Velanie? She'd be more apt to kill Jason. I still say Celia Grant's the one. She must have gone back there to see Velanie while everybody was at lunch and—"

"So did Arnold Wynn go back there. I checked with the instructor who saw him soon after they went in to lunch. She was sitting so she could watch him go down the hall."

"Well, of course he went down the hall. He told me so himself. But he heard Velanie talking to somebody, so he didn't go in."

"Where the hell has Wynn been all afternoon? I've had a state trooper looking for him all over the place. I'd better go have a talk with him right now."

He made a halfhearted move to get up, but was glad to let Lucy dissuade him.

"Wynn is still all shaken up and he's working something out in his mind, so don't rush him before he's ready, or he'll clam up the way he did with me. Anyway, he promised to see you after dinner." She knew she was making it sound more positive than Wynn had, but this was the

173

moment for a slight exaggeration. And the moment to make another drink.

She wanted to ask McDougal if he'd located his ex-wife and checked her alibi, but pride—or was it vanity?—wouldn't let her.

Halfway through the second drink, McDougal said, "By the way, Eileen was at the hairdresser's from eleven to one. She left me a note when she checked out of the Inn—I thought you might like to see it."

Lucy said just as casually, "I'm glad that's cleared up," and didn't even reach for the envelope McDougal was holding out. He had to get up from the chaise to give it to her.

She glanced at the handwriting and thought, Backhand. And curly capitals. Finishing school and never outgrew it.

Dear Mac,

I know you'll come back to Wingate in a hurry now that there's been a killing—that irresistible lure. And just in case Jason is involved, I'm clearing out to save you embarrassment. This has sobered me up considerably. As the ex-wife of an inspector of homicide, I don't think it would be seemly—lovely word, "seemly"—to be involved, even for drinks, with Velanie's husband. My guess is that he's now your favorite suspect. At least you and I never considered killing each other. Or did you? If so, I wouldn't really blame you.

Your quasi-reformed sinner,

Eileen

P.S. If you want to reach me, I'll be in New York at the Plaza.

Lucy handed the note back without comment. She didn't want to risk saying anything for fear of saying too

174

much. McDougal took out his lighter, struck it, and put the flame to a corner of the note, holding it over a large ashtray embossed with *Do You Really Want To Smoke?*

"Probably safer not to toss it into a wastebasket."

Lucy understood what he was telling her. All she said was "You're mucking up my only big ashtray," but there was an undercurrent of laughter.

"Yoo-hoo, Mrs. Ramsdale?"

"Out here."

Mavis, the gangly maid, appeared in the doorway to the terrace carrying a tray covered with see-through plastic wrap. "Chef Ronda thought you'd like something to nibble on with your drinks."

Whatever Chef Ronda had said, he certainly hadn't said "something to nibble on." Lucy and McDougal glanced at each other and kept their faces straight.

"How nice, Mavis. This is Inspector McDougal, who's in charge of the case."

Mavis, staring with unabashed interest, tilted the tray precariously.

"Put it down here on the table. And please thank Chef Ronda for me." Lucy glanced at the contents of the tray. "Oh, lovely. Mac, do have one while they're hot."

"I nearly stepped on your painting when I was coming in," Mavis said. "The one you showed me with the joggers this morning. Whoever left it there on the floor half under the door was awful careless. A good thing it had a cover on it."

McDougal shot up from his chair like a jack-in-the-box. "Where is it?"

"On the bed."

He loped into the bedroom.

"Hilda Simms must have had it," Lucy called after him.

She was flattered that McDougal was so eager to see her work, and she couldn't resist going in after him to get his reaction.

McDougal was holding the Pliofilm-covered sketch in both hands, and staring at it so oddly that Lucy said, "Don't you like it?"

McDougal went on staring, and Lucy came over to take a look herself.

"Oh, goddammit, somebody got water on the middle of the jogger's suit. It's faded to pink. Look at that; I'll have to try to paint over it."

"Not just yet," the inspector said. "I'd like to have it tested first."

"Tested! Mac, you can't think the paint is poisonous."

"Not poisonous. But we may find traces of blood where the spot was washed off."

As Mavis said in the kitchen later, to a fascinated audience, " 'Blood,' the inspector says. It was just like a TV show. And Mrs. Ramsdale turning pale as a ghost and moaning."

Lucy hadn't moaned. She had let out one small whimper before she said, "Thank you, Mavis. That will be all."

She didn't ask how blood could have got on her sketch. With her strong visual imagination, she didn't need to. It was horribly clear. McDougal urged her to go home, but she said to hell with that, she'd be more use where she was.

She revived considerably over the veal and curried fruit, but she finished less than half her dinner. "I can't hurt that nice chef's feelings, Mac. You'll have to smuggle the rest of this out in a briefcase or something."

McDougal himself wasn't eating too avidly. He was re-

membering something Chef Ronda had said about one of
the possible suspects, and he thought he saw a connection
between that and what he was sure was a dabbed-off bloodstain on Lucy's sketch. But it wasn't good table talk, not
tonight, and he didn't want to leave Lucy alone till she
acted more like herself.

They were still on the terrace when somewhere near a
dog began howling. Lucy said, "That damn thing sounds
like a werewolf. Let's go indoors to have our coffee." She
had picked up the thermos of coffee when Sergeant Terrizi
came running across the lawn to the terrace.

"A trooper just found the body."

"Whose body?" McDougal said.

Terrizi seemed not to hear. He was staring at them
glassily.

"Nicky, drink this." Lucy held out her half-filled glass
of wine.

Terrizi took one gulp. "I'm sorry. I'm being a baby. But
first Velanie and then this—"

"Now if you'd tell us what 'this' is." McDougal said.
"Who was killed?"

Lucy said, "It was Arnold Wynn, wasn't it? I'm afraid
he asked for it."

11

THE INSPECTOR was being deliberately tough. "This is no time for the hair-shirt act." He saw Lucy stiffen and thought, Good, let her get mad. "If you want a session later on who's to blame for Wynn's death, then I'll take top prize. But right now I'd rather catch a murderer and I need both of you."

Sergeant Terrizi's eyes looked suddenly shinier. Lucy said in a shaky voice, "Just don't ask me to look at another corpse. One viewing a day is my motto."

The inspector had no intention of letting her see Wynn's corpse. Terrizi had said, "He was in that little woods behind the tennis court. A trooper was patrolling the grounds with a police dog and found him. The poison must have been in his flask. He'd dropped it beside him when—" The sergeant's voice had trailed off, as if he couldn't bear to describe the indescribable. McDougal had shooed them indoors and had only taken time to call headquarters and to alert the troopers already on guard.

Now he said to Lucy, "Terrizi's already identified the

body. I want you for something more talkative. Find the secretary, Hilda Simms, and pump her for all you're worth. You'll get much more out of her than I could."

When Lucy nodded in agreement, McDougal knew she was on the road to recovery. "Find out if Wynn went to her office this afternoon. Did he ask about Velanie's will? Did he quiz her the way he quizzed you? Feel your way. I've seen your radar finder working before. And when you've finished, come right back here so I'll know where to reach you. After I see the police doctor and get things under way, I'll be in the dietitian's office. And I may need your help with interviews."

"Since when?" Lucy smiled faintly. "You just want to keep an eye on me." But she didn't sound indignant.

"My guess is that Simms would have gone right back to her office after dinner. Sergeant, will you drop Lucy off there? Or stay with her till you locate Simms."

Terrizi got the unspoken message: *Lucy will be safe with Simms.*

"And then get hold of Celia Grant and Jason and bring them to me. In chains, if necessary."

Ten minutes later, having deposited Lucy in Simms's office, Terrizi was blasting the trooper who'd been left to guard Jason at the cottage. "You didn't even look in his room every half hour to make sure?"

The trooper was aggrieved. "But I took him in his supper just a while ago. Around seven-thirty. And I didn't leave the door even for a minute. I had a maid bring over the tray."

"If he was well enough to eat, he was well enough to be interviewed. You should have called the inspector."

"All he ate was a little soup and a cracker." The trooper

179

neglected to mention that he himself had polished off the rest of the meal, in addition to sandwiches.

"And that gave him strength to leap out a window and slide down a drainpipe. I should have taken away his clothes. Not that he'd mind running around in the raw, waving his pecker at the ladies. God knows when I'll track him down again. Check with the chauffeur—he lives over the garage—and find out if any cars are missing."

Celia was as unfindable as Jason. Terrizi tried her cottage first: empty. He then tried to get into the main house by the back way to check her office, but the back door was locked. When he loped around to the front, the trooper on duty said no one had gone in or out. "Two white-haired ladies wanted to go out and jog by moonlight"—his tone expressed what he thought of that idea—"but I wouldn't let 'em."

"We already have enough wacks running loose." Terrizi described his two missing suspects. "If you see one or both of them, use your walkie-talkie but don't budge from this door. We've got more men coming, so you'll be relieved before too long."

He had started down the hall when he happened to glance into an open doorway and froze in astonishment. Just inside was a woman kneeling, bent over backward, with her head dangling toward her legs behind. As he stared, she brought her head up, saw him through streaming hair, and said in a panting voice, "Jackrabbit."

Was she mad? He was even more baffled because she looked vaguely familiar.

"Usually do it in my room, but tonight we're all sticking together as long as we can."

Now he saw three more women sitting on the floor at his left, rocking back and forth on their buttocks before a

TV screen. In the solarium just beyond, four women sat at a card table. He heard "Double five clubs" just as a man's voice shouted, "Freeze where you are, you bastard!"

The sergeant reached instinctively for his gun before he realized the man's voice came from the television set. He felt silly but relieved.

Jackrabbit was grinning. "Even the police are jumpy tonight. Did you find Arnold Wynn?"

So they'd already heard. "A trooper found the body."

"The body! How long ago? Where? Got any leads on who did it?" She flip-flopped her hair back from her face and Terrizi knew now why Jackrabbit looked familiar: Marta Galt, the TV interviewer. Torn between pleasure over the story he'd have to tell Angie and annoyance because he'd been tricked, he said, "We're working on it."

"I'll phone in a bulletin for the eleven-o'clock news. How do you spell your name?"

The TV was making so much noise he almost had to shout to be heard. ". . . and the name of the state trooper who found the body is Cooper, Ivan Cooper."

"Short for Ivanhoe?"

Terrizi grinned, for the first time that evening. "For Ivanovitch. Polish. And his girl isn't named Rebecca."

"All right, we're even. How was he killed? Not Ivanovitch—Wynn."

"Poisoned."

"Which means a dame did it."

The sergeant shrugged. "Maybe—maybe not."

"Wanna bet? Have you questioned Celia Grant yet?"

"I'm looking for her now." Terrizi's conscience prickled; he shouldn't be standing here yakking. "Have you seen her?"

"She was in here right after dinner being the gracious

new Madame. Later I saw her out the window. And who should go by awhile later, headed the same way, but the grieving widower."

"Jason?" Terrizi quivered all over.

"None other. After all, Celia's rich now. Or she soon will be. And Jason will need a new moneybag, so it's time to get cozy."

They're already cozy. Terrizi was glad to know more of the inside story than Marta Galt, and determined not to give it away. "Which way was he—"

"Oh, good evening, Officer. How nice of you to watch over us." One of the buttocks rockers had turned and was smiling at him; it was hay-hair, whom he'd seen in the back corridor that afternoon. He almost didn't recognize her because her hair was now sleek and silvery blond.

"Good evening, ma'am." Remembering the inspector's warning not to panic the inmates, Terrizi was doing his best to sound stolidly pleasant.

"There'll be more than one of you on guard, won't there?"

"Yes, ma'am. The inspector just ordered more reinforcements, so we'll be all over the place. You needn't worry."

Marta Galt winked at him but didn't give him away. Evidently she was saving her tidbit on the second killing for her network's eleven-o'clock news.

The sleeked-up hay-hair swiveled to face the screen again; her two companions on the floor hadn't even turned around. They were absorbed in a killing of their own, and rocking faster and faster in time to the background music.

Picking up where he'd left off, Terrizi asked Marta Galt again, "Which way were they going?"

"That way." She flapped her hand toward the right. "If you catch up with Jason, belt him one for me. But he isn't the one you want. Jason wouldn't use poison, not even on a rat. And believe me, he's not a woman."

"Poor Arnold," Hilda Simms said. "He wasn't any use any more, so I suppose it doesn't matter he's dead. Not even to him. He was such a nuisance this afternoon when I was making the overseas calls, hanging around wanting to know how much Velanie had left him."

Lucy wriggled forward in her seat trying to get her feet on the floor, but the chair was too high. The secretary got up instantly, fetched a small stool from the corner, and knelt to put it under Lucy's feet. "There, now you'll be comfier."

Lucy came near laughing hysterically. It was such a ridiculous word—"comfier"—and especially tonight. "Did you tell him anything about the will?"

Hilda Simms looked troubled. "I wasn't going to. I thought he'd been through enough for one day, and the lawyer would have told him sometime after the funeral. And anyway, I hoped Madame would have been more generous in the final draft. She was like that—give or grab—you never knew from one minute to the next. And it was really so unfair. Helga, the operator who gives facials here—she's been with Velanie forever, but to leave her more money than Arnold seems really mean. All he got, in the draft I saw after Velanie's sister died, was the same monthly allowance he's been getting for years. But Arnold kept pestering me till I got so exasperated I told him straight out."

"How did he react?"

"He made an odd face." The secretary attempted to imitate Arnold's odd face, but Lucy couldn't tell from the contortions whether Wynn had been hurt or enraged.

"Then he said, 'Maybe Velanie got what she deserved.' But if he didn't do it, why would he kill himself?"

Lucy was about to say, He didn't—he just brought it on himself trying blackmail. But Hilda Simms looked so exhausted she decided that could wait. "Did Arnold ask if you'd heard Velanie talking to someone this noon?"

"Yes, but of course I couldn't have. I was at the Oaks then, waiting for that woman."

"You'll be relieved to know Mrs. Torrance left town this afternoon."

"She put it off too long." Simms sounded bitter. "When I think of Madame having to worry about her this morning . . . Jason caused even more trouble than Arnold did. But I'm afraid that was more Madame's fault than his. The more she cut him down, the more he needed to get on top. I don't mean sexually, though there's that, too."

It wasn't entirely a non sequitur that Lucy thought of a piece of detection she could do lying down.

Simms had nothing more to tell about Arnold Wynn's visit that afternoon. "The call I'd placed to Tokyo, to the manager of our salon there, came through and Arnold left while I was still on the phone."

"Did he give you any idea of where he was going?"

Simms said he hadn't. "But I know he was in Mrs. Vining's office for a few minutes right afterward. I heard her talking to him so soothingly. With all she has on her mind, it shows how kind and thoughtful she is."

And I'm a stinker, Lucy thought. I haven't been near her since just after we found Velanie. "Do you know where Adele is now?"

"At the nursing home. Her husband was much worse again, but Mrs. Vining couldn't go out there till after the press conference. She set it up at the Oaks so we wouldn't have reporters and photographers swarming in here. How Madame would have loved to read about herself. I should think she'll be a front-page story even in Europe."

Lucy said absently, "Unless somebody lets loose a nuclear blast."

"I was at the barracks tonight when you called about Wynn, Inspector, so I came back to see if there was anything I could do." Detective Carlin thought it unnecessary to mention he'd been playing gin rummy and losing so heavily he'd been glad of an excuse to drop out of the game. The black circles around his eyes were more pronounced this evening, and the effect was even more raccoonish because Carlin needed a shave and looked furry.

McDougal, noticing this, was grateful for the brief flash of amusement. He had just come from seeing Wynn's body, and it had hit him all the harder because he still felt partly responsible. "It was poison this time," he told Carlin. "Somebody'd put it in his flask. From the looks of him, the doctor thinks cyanide. We'll know better tomorrow. Poor old drunk. I gather liquor was poison to him, but this time he got more than he bargained for."

"I hope the little lady—Mrs. Ramsdale—didn't find this one."

The inspector said he was thankful she hadn't. "One of our men was patrolling the grounds with a police dog, and the dog started making a din." He remembered Lucy shivering, in the warm night air, saying, "It sounds like a werewolf."

He said now, "She was already upset enough."

"I sure wish I could have found her sketch for her."

"It came back tonight." He told Carlin about the washed-off bloodstain. "Somebody went to a lot of trouble.

Even covered the whole thing neatly with a sheet of transparent Pliofilm."

Detective Carlin wasn't the quickest of thinkers, but "transparent Pliofilm" did stir a faint recollection. "The cleaning lady here was telling me . . ." He repeated the cleaning woman's remark about "see-through paper." "Almost a whole roll thrown away. In somebody's wastebasket or something."

"Get hold of the housekeeper again and have her help you locate the cleaning woman. Find out which office or room she found it in. This may be a real lead. I'm glad you thought of it."

In the warm glow of praise received, Carlin's memory cells churned anew. "You said an old drunk. Did he look kind of seedy and with white hair flapping down around his neck?"

The dead man had looked worse than seedy by the time McDougal saw him, but the description of the hair fitted. "You saw him? When?"

McDougal's long face looked even more bony, almost gaunt, as he heard Carlin's answer. "You couldn't know we were looking for him. I should have told you. My guess is that somebody arranged to meet him in that clump of woods so as to get Wynn out of the way and keep him from talking to me or anybody else. Probably promised to bring him whatever blackmail money he'd asked for. But the poison must have been put in his flask earlier. If he hung around back there waiting—and the killer would have planned it that way—Wynn was pretty sure to take a drink. Then, curtains. Too bad he can't make a curtain speech."

Sergeant Terrizi was on his way to double-check with the chauffeur about any missing car when he heard the plop and splash of what sounded like a fish jumping. His mind, occupied with other matters, registered vaguely, A damn big fish, then sharpened to attention: the pond he'd seen earlier was in front of the main house. This sound had come from somewhere much nearer. Swimming pool—that was it. He ran over and peered into the nearest side of the glass-enclosed building.

The pool was dimly lit around the edges, a pale glow like a pinkish night-light, but Jason was clearly visible, posed on the diving board in swimming trunks.

The crazy bastard, Terrizi thought almost affectionately, and raced around to the front to get in, but the door was locked. When the sergeant banged, Jason paid no attention. He rose in the air in a double somersault, dived—no splashing like a big fish this time—and swam down the pool toward the back.

The sergeant wrapped his right fist in a handkerchief, smashed the glass beside the lock in the door, pulled back the bolt, and ran in.

"Get out of there!" he bellowed.

Jason turned onto his back and floated. "Come on in. Very refreshing." But as the sergeant started to yank off his pants, Jason swam to the edge and pulled himself out. "I'd hate to see a cop all wet. Sorry, that was a stupid crack. Did you want something?"

The sergeant used a pungent phrase seldom heard on television. ". . . and you're coming along with me right now, to the inspector."

"In this?" Jason indicated his dripping trunks. "I came over to clear my head, but if I have to be hauled in I'd rather go clothed in my dignity. Let's stop by the cottage and pick up my clothes."

"You'd have been smart to stay where you were in bed, with a trooper on guard. This way, you have no alibi."

"You already knew that. I told you this afternoon."

"I mean for tonight."

"What happened tonight?" Jason had dropped the bantering tone. He looked tense.

"Wynn's dead. Poisoned. As if you didn't know." But even while Terrizi said it, he was remembering Marta Galt's "Jason wouldn't use poison." And however exasperated the sergeant felt, he had a hunch she was right.

For one thing, Jason was turning green. As he leaned over and retched, the spirit of Mrs. Terrizi made her son moan, "Not in the pool."

Jason, who may have had a Greek mother of a similarly fussy nature, pulled himself up, put a hand to his mouth, and bolted into the passageway. The sergeant raced to catch up, but Jason wasn't going anywhere. He was too busy being sick into the antiseptic footbath.

He was still looking pale ten minutes later when Terrizi delivered him to the inspector and went off to find Celia Grant.

McDougal had had a mental picture of a second-rate, slick-haired Romeo, a picture perhaps colored negatively by Lucy's having said, "He's quite good-looking. I wanted to sketch him."

But the Jason standing in front of his desk was no slick-haired Romeo but a horse of quite another color—more like a magnificent stallion exhausted after a race. The man was startlingly beautiful, in a plain white T-shirt and blue jeans, and with his black curls still wet and uncombed.

He sat down in the chair on the other side of the desk and said quietly, "Inspector, I've made you a lot of trouble and it doesn't help to say I'm sorry. I've behaved like an idiot but I didn't kill Velanie and I didn't kill Wynn. I went off this afternoon and got drunk because I've always

188

taken the easy way out. Now I'm sober and I'm through running. I'll tell you whatever I know."

What he knew was pretty much what McDougal had already guessed. Celia had not been alone at noon. "I took her back to the cottage and stayed there an hour or so. She'd come over to the pool in near hysterics after she'd seen Velanie and heard about my supposed affair with Mrs. Torrance, which, by the way, consisted of having one drink with the lady."

"So I heard. Are you sure Celia wasn't in a state because Velanie had found out about her affair with you?"

Jason was silent a moment. "The last time I saw Velanie, around ten-thirty this morning, she was madder at Wynn for what she called his 'cock-and-bull story' than she was at me. And I didn't mind her bawling me out, because I was so relieved she hadn't bought Wynn's story. I may as well tell you right now it wasn't Celia who inveigled me into an affair. I got her into it to amuse myself"—he grimaced—"so I'm partly responsible for whatever she may have done today. If I were a noble character, I'd say I killed Velanie and Wynn and take the rap, but I have a primitive instinct to save my own neck."

McDougal got out a pack of Kents. "Cigarette?"

"Thanks, I don't smoke. Bad for the wind."

The inspector's mouth twitched as he bit back a smile. Jason noticed and said wryly, "I'm great on the minor virtues."

It was hard not to like the man. "I gather you can't alibi Celia for the entire period from, say, eleven-thirty this morning to one?"

Jason picked his words carefully. "From just after eleven-thirty to around twelve-fifteen, yes, for sure. I went to sleep after that. You can guess what we'd been doing. It

189

was the only way to calm Celia down. I didn't wake up till around one, when the phone rang. Switchboard calling Celia to tell her about Velanie. Celia was already dressed. I leaped into my clothes and left by the back way, and went right to the office. And when I saw Velanie, the way she looked, I never despised myself more. I felt as if I'd caused it."

"You think Celia went back there while you were sleeping and killed your wife?"

"I was hell-bent on believing Wynn did it. But now that he's been killed, too, where else is there to go?"

"If Velanie finally believed Wynn's story and called Celia back there late this morning to accuse her, couldn't that be the real reason Celia was in such a state when she came to the pool? Maybe it wasn't really Mrs. Torrance she was upset about." (He was glad to find he could say "Mrs. Torrance" so impersonally.) "Maybe it was because she'd just killed her benefactor to keep from losing everything she'd counted on."

There were at least two flaws in this scenario; the inspector found it interesting that his listener didn't spot them.

Jason said slowly, "That's what I've been trying not to think about. If I made love to the girl soon after—" He couldn't finish. "Mind if I go back to my room?"

McDougal didn't mind. "But don't tell anybody about Wynn for now. I mean that very seriously. And don't leave by the window again, or you'll be in real trouble."

"I'm already in it. Look, couldn't you send all the biddies home tomorrow? They can't have had anything to do with the murders, and the idea of having them around for underwater exercises, weeping phony tears for 'poor Mr. Velanie'—I'm apt to drown them."

For reasons of his own, McDougal wanted the biddies around awhile longer. "Get one of the other instructors to take over your class. She'll explain that the grieving widower is in seclusion."

"Don't turn the screws any tighter. What you won't believe—because I can hardly believe it myself—is that I feel terrible about Velanie."

"Cheer up. You may inherit some of her money. And in case you don't, you'd do well to play up to some of the richest biddies while you have them around to work on."

"That's a rotten crack." Jason got up abruptly. "It beats me why Mrs. Ramsdale likes you."

The inspector was already feeling rather ashamed of himself. "Sometimes it beats me, too." He could understand now why Lucy wanted to sketch Jason, but she'd never asked to sketch him, McDougal, and that rankled. He knew he was being childish. To atone, he said, "Try to get a decent sleep. If it's any consolation, Velanie was the only one responsible for getting herself killed."

Terrizi appeared almost as soon as Jason had gone. "You want me to put a trooper on him again? Not that it did any good before."

McDougal said he thought Jason would stay put for the night. "Did you find Celia Grant?"

Terrizi scowled. "I know where she is, but we can't get at her till tomorrow." He said Celia Grant had gone to the infirmary over the ex-stables around eight o'clock, complaining of chills and fever; the nurse had put her to bed there and had refused to let the sergeant wake her. Terrizi had left a man on guard outside the door.

"She won't go anywhere tonight. She's scared."

For the next ten minutes, McDougal talked about his ideas on the case while Terrizi's young face ran the gamut of emotions from Z to A. Finally Terrizi said, "What put you on to it?"

"Kipling." McDougal was enjoying himself. "And my Scottish grandmother. She used to read me a book of his called *Kim*. You know it?"

Terrizi had to admit he didn't.

"Most people don't any more. Kim had to glance at all the objects in a room—or on, say, a table—and memorize them instantly so he could recall the whole lot later. I thought that was quite a trick when I was seven or eight, so I practiced it all over the place. Until it became automatic." He saw the rapt look on Terrizi's face—the I'll-learn-to-observe-like-that—and part of him was flattered. Another part of him jeered, You're sounding off like a politician, and it made him say aloud, "I've been inexcusably slow. This afternoon I read those idiotic memos on food"—he gestured to the wallboard—"instead of concentrating on the case. But tonight I thought back and did a Kim, reconstructing. And I spotted what I'd missed before. I'd seen it but hadn't reacted. I went over and took another look and I'm quite sure that's the answer, but I can't prove it yet with the evidence wiped out. By the way, for now, Wynn was a suicide."

Terrizi gaped. "With the poison in his flask?"

"We needn't mention the flask. We'll just give out that it's suicide."

The sergeant leaped up. "Oh, my God! Marta Galt!" He gabbled an explanation. "Eleven-o'clock news. I'll have to stop her."

"I hope you can. It's important. You've got fifty minutes."

Marta was still on her knees in the lounge, bent over backward. When Sergeant Terrizi tapped her on the only portion of her anatomy available, her stomach, she let out a squeak, then struggled to pull her head up, and gasped, "You nearly gave me a heart attack. Got more news?"

"Wynn's death was suicide. Did you phone your network yet?"

"There's no phone in here. I was putting it off as long as I could." She looked at him shrewdly. "There's something phony about this. How come you thought first he was killed and now you've switched to suicide?"

Terrizi muttered something about tests proving the police had been wrong.

"You're a lousy liar. You're trying to con me."

"Look, you've got to go along." In desperation, he knelt on the floor beside her. "If you break that story on the news tonight, I'll be in bad trouble. I blabbed out of turn."

"You blabbed to the wrong gal. I'm not giving up an exclusive just to bail you out."

Terrizi thought fast. "Go ahead. Wreck my whole career. I was going to get married this fall but now I'll be out of a job."

Marta Galt's face had softened. "You're getting married?"

"I was." He sounded somber.

"I suppose one more day wouldn't matter. How soon can you break the case? Remember, I get first crack. Ramsdale already promised."

"Oh, you will. You will." The sergeant was so grateful he warbled. "I'll bless you forever. We'll send you an invitation to the wedding." As soon as he'd heard what he'd said, he was embarrassed. "Not that I'd expect you to come."

"Why? If I'm not off on my honeymoon." Marta Galt sat back on her heels and said dreamily, "We think maybe Iceland. My guy's got a thing about fjords."

193

Detective Carlin had gone in a straight line this evening, and was already reporting back to McDougal. "I got the cleaning lady on the phone and she said she found the see-through roll of paper in a wastebasket. It was in the second room from the back elevator on this floor, called Mirage Ruby or something like that. The name's on the door."

At ten-forty, a trooper brought a note from Terrizi scrawled on the back of a bridge score. "Am staying with M.G. in the lounge awhile longer—taking no chances on her getting to a phone. She's teaching me Yoga."

Several minutes later McDougal, on his way down the corridor to Lucy's room, came to the second door from the elevator and stopped to look at the name: "Maharajah's Ruby." He decided he liked Mirage Ruby better: it fitted the place—and the murderer.

When he knocked on Lucy's door, it swung open as if it hadn't been properly shut and revealed a nerve-racking sight: Lucy lay stretched out on her bed like a corpse, with her arms folded across her chest and a ghostly grayish-white stuff all over her face and throat.

The inspector was so appalled he couldn't move for at least three seconds; then he made it in two leaps to the bed.

"Does my voice sound muzzy with this gop on?" Lucy had opened her eyes and was looking at him with interest.

Her voice had never sounded so charming, or so welcome, to McDougal. But the cop in him understood instantly that she was trying some kind of experiment connected with Velanie's murder. "Say some more. Keep on talking."

"Jason Pappas picked a peck of pickled peppers—red hot," Lucy said. "I sound the same to myself and I've had

194

it on just over fifteen minutes. My God, I'd better peel it off right now before I'm encased in cement."

McDougal watched with manly trepidation as she took hold of the still pliable substance by the two top corners and yanked. The mask made a sucking sound and came off in one piece.

"It's not as bad as ripping off adhesive tape," Lucy assured him. She slathered her face in cream from a jar on her bedside table and wiped it off with a tissue. Then she propped up the pillows behind her and leaned back looking rosily refreshed.

"If it had hardened as much as Velanie's, my whole face would have been too stiff to talk so you could understand me. So that means she couldn't have made that phone call to us herself. She was already dead. Why the hell were we so slow to catch on?"

The inspector decided it wasn't the time to say, *You were slow.*

He said Lucy had made an important discovery.

"You're stalling. You never say things like 'important discovery.' Don't you think I'm right?"

McDougal, picking his words carefully, said, "Up to a point."

"Then what's bothering you? You still sound cagey."

"Could Celia have imitated Velanie's voice that well?"

"Why not? She knew Velanie better than anyone else except the secretary. And she hated Wynn's guts." Lucy stopped and considered. " 'Guts' is a funny word to use for Wynn. It's Celia who has guts enough for an elephant. Jason's no match for her out of bed."

McDougal said they'd been in bed together that noon. "But Jason can't alibi Celia for the entire time, because he went to sleep afterward."

195

"He probably snores. It's so irritating to have a man snore then. Of course, not if you want to sneak out while he sleeps, and kill somebody. What kind of alibi does she have for tonight?"

"She's been in the infirmary since eight this evening. But we don't know yet when Wynn died. The lab hasn't finished the analysis. And for now we're putting out the word it was suicide. Let the killer think the cops are stupid."

"Simms already thinks so." Lucy saw McDougal's expression and laughed. "I mean, she thinks it was suicide because she's not really thinking. How about Marta Galt? Will she buy it?"

"Terrizi has Galt muzzled again."

"She'll chew off the muzzle if we don't soon give her a—" Lucy was yawning unashamedly. "I'm folding right now. Don't forget to water the beds out front before you come back in the morning."

The inspector said he wouldn't forget. There were at least two other things he was much more determined not to forget than flower beds, but he didn't mention them.

If Lucy had wakened in the night and wandered out on her terrace, she would have been surprised to find a trooper standing guard, or sitting. He left before even so early a bird as Lucy could rise and catch him.

196

12

MᴄDᴏᴜɢᴀʟ ᴡᴏᴋᴇ ᴜᴘ around six feeling as if he'd been pummeled and jabbed all night long. It was the first time he'd slept in the studio without Lucy being in her house a hundred yards away, and it was a measure of how low he felt that he boiled water for instant coffee instead of his usual brew—strong—poured through a Chemex filter. When he took his cup into the big main studio room, the sun flooding in seemed an affront. Murky gray drizzle would have been more in keeping with his mood.

A shower and shave didn't improve matters, but his head cleared enough to remember he was supposed to water the flower beds out front.

The garden hose was attached to a faucet on the edge of the terrace, and McDougal had a fetish about keeping it wound in neat coils between usings. This morning when he found it sprawled out every which way on the lawn, instead of being exasperated by Lucy's casual habits he blamed himself because he'd gone to New York and left her with all the chores.

He was adjusting the nozzle to spray when a dream he'd

had the night before suddenly surfaced: Lucy standing by the zinnias saying, "I need a touch of red in my bouquet, so water them with blood."

This only sharpened his edginess. He was in such a hurry to get to the spa that he turned on the hose full blast and flushed a small rabbit, which stared at him reproachfully before hopping to drier quarters.

When he walked onto Lucy's terrace a half hour later, it gave him a start to see her hold up her brush, bright with crimson, in greeting.

"Let me finish this flower before it dries. I knew if I didn't get back on the horse and ride, I'd never want to use red again."

He had never liked her more. And he felt even worse about not telling her how his ideas on the case were shaping up, but she was safer this way.

He watched her at work and noticed her wristwatch was pushed halfway up her arm. "I should have taken another link or two out of your watchband. I'll do it when we get home."

Lucy said "Hmm" absently, and he shut up.

When she laid down her brush several minutes later and said "There," in a satisfied tone, he took it as his cue to go over and look at the sketch on her pad. It was the one she'd begun the day before in class: little figures upside down on the Yoga boards, with a bouquet of flowers à la Chagall in one corner. "Charming" wasn't a word he usually tangled with, but he brought it out for the occasion.

"It is good, isn't it? And it's helped me exorcise the haunts. Or at least make them back off. Did you remember to water the zinnias?"

"Almost drowned them. And a rabbit." When Lucy got on her damn-those-rabbits expression McDougal felt more back to normal. "I'll use the rabbit repellent again next week."

"If we're home by then. I woke up last night around three feeling low as hell, and I cheered myself up planning what we'll have for dinner the first night we're home."

"What are we having?" He began to feel genuinely hungry.

"It's a surprise. Did you have any breakfast?"

"Instant coffee," he said, in the tone of a man enjoying martyrdom but needing sympathy to sustain it.

Lucy reacted appropriately. "I'll ask Chef Ronda to send breakfast over to your office."

Chef Ronda didn't send breakfast; he brought it himself to the dietitian's office: scrambled eggs with anchovies, and a pot of real coffee. And he brought a bit of information that sharpened the inspector's appetite.

Ronda said he'd heard from Mavis about Mrs. Ramsdale's sketch being returned with a bloodstain washed off and a Pliofilm covering. He'd remembered then that one of the kitchen boys had got out a new roll of Pliofilm to wrap up the roast-beef sandwiches for Mrs. Ramsdale, around one-thirty the day before. The reason Ronda had remembered, he said, was that "rater the boy comprain somebody had snitched it. Then creaning woman brings it back yesterday in rate afternoon, says she found in waste-basket in a crient's room. I think, New kind of kreptomaniac, taking paper. But after I hear Mavis's story this morning, I ask boy if he see anybody in kitchen or pantry not of staff, around time Priofim disappeared. And he say Miss Grant comes to ask them to carry on as before, now that Madame is dead. Can't wait to show she is boss rady." Ronda made an *ugh* face. "Or she needs excuse to grab the Priofim after staff go off."

"Anyone else?"

Ronda's cross look evaporated. "Mrs. Vining must have sent a maid to ret me know she cannot be in for dinner because she go to nursing home. She say how sorry she is not to be here on such a difficut night, but she knows how I cope with any emergency. I find her sweet note when I return from session with you."

McDougal said that was very helpful. He showed his appreciation more graphically by polishing off the whole plateful of scrambled eggs.

It was fortunate he had this sustenance before Officer Willoughby appeared, fresh as an unfolding daisy, and full of information on the two matters McDougal had asked him to pump Celia Grant's secretary about.

Miss Grant, Willoughby said, had seen Madame Velanie twice the morning before. The first time she'd come back to her office in high spirits. "Mary said Miss Grant wasn't putting it on the way she sometimes did. She was so pleased she sort of chattered on about Madame showing her the sketch Mrs. Ramsdale had done. Madame said they'd have a top designer do new costumes like the ones in the sketch. And they're going to send out a fancy booklet using a lot more of the drawings. Madame was going to have Mrs. Ramsdale get to work on them right away. Mary says Madame had threatened sometimes to close the spa because it was running in the red, and when Miss Grant had wanted better-looking exercise costumes, Madame had refused every time because it would cost too much, but now she gave Miss Grant cart blanch."

The inspector savored, briefly, the blanched cart.

Willoughby was still pouring out his nuggets. Madame had called Miss Grant the second time around ten-forty-five. "She called on the house phone herself, so that meant her secretary wasn't around, and she asked Miss

Grant to come right over. And when Miss Grant came back the second time she looked terribly upset, and she went right out again without saying where. Usually she was very careful to let Mary know where she could be reached, because Madame expected people to be on call. But Miss Grant was gone for almost two hours this time. The switchboard finally reached her in her cottage to tell her about Madame."

McDougal got out a cigarette, which Officer Willoughby leaped to light with a match. He accepted one himself, but he smoked it in little puffs and spurts without inhaling.

"And what about the urgent message Mary sent downstairs yesterday, asking Mrs. Vining to come to Celia Grant's office?"

Willoughby said that whenever Miss Simms and Mrs. Vining were both out of their offices, all their outside calls were put through to Celia Grant's secretary. "Mary keeps a record of the calls to give Miss Simms, but the one for Mrs. Vining from the nursing home sounded so important she wanted to locate her fast."

McDougal couldn't say what he was thinking, so he said, "Mary sounds like a girl who uses her head."

Officer Willoughby agreed radiantly. "She has a Ph.D. in psychology, but teaching jobs are very scarce and research departments are using computers instead of trained people. . . ." Willoughby was eager to give Mary's opinion of this menacing trend, and the inspector had to be tactful in leading him back to the phone call.

"Mary never found out what it was about, because Mrs. Vining rushed right back to her own office to return the call. But it had to be important because the doctor had phoned himself. Mary had taken calls before from the nursing home, but it was always a nurse or a secretary. So she figured if a doctor dialed a number himself it must be a real emergency."

"I'd heard you were sick in the infirmary." Lucy couldn't quite keep the skepticism out of her voice. Celia Grant looked revoltingly healthy; standing there in the brilliant sunlight on the terrace, she looked like the sort of ingénue who used to come on stage swinging a racket and calling, "Anyone for tennis?"

Celia wasn't carrying a racket but her costume would have been fitting for a love–all match: shorts and a halter again. She said all she'd needed was a real night's rest. "I had to get away from people."

Especially police, Lucy thought sourly. If you finished off Arnold Wynn after Velanie, no wonder you needed a rest.

"Oh, you've already done another!" Celia had spotted the sketch of the Yoga upside-downers, propped up against a water glass to dry. "How wonderful. If only Madame could have seen this one. She didn't get a chance to tell you herself, but she was already planning a direct-mail brochure using lots and lots of your sketches."

Lucy, usually attuned to praise, was listening to Celia's voice more than to the artificially sweetened words. Could Celia have changed it that much to imitate Velanie on the phone?

". . . and Madame adored the costumes you put on the joggers in your first sketch. She'd already asked me to have new exercise suits made using your design."

Is that why you washed off the bloodstains so carefully? You needed that sketch.

Celia was still talking. ". . . and I leave it to you to

decide on a fee. Because I know your original arrangement with Madame was just a week of treatments here. Oh, I nearly forgot. The operator who gives facials asked me when you'd like a first appointment."

So I'll look refreshed for the funerals? Lucy was about to snarl an answer when she remembered Hilda Simms talking about the operator who'd been with Madame for years, and who had been left a bigger bequest in the will than Arnold Wynn. Might be useful to talk to her—about the beauty mask, for one thing. "This morning will be fine. Anytime between eleven and one, if she's free." It was after ten then.

"Let's say eleven-thirty. I'll see that she's free."

Queen of all you survey now. You must feel home safe. "That was a fast recovery you made from your—" Lucy paused deliberately—"your illness."

Celia wasn't the kind who looked flustered, but she showed it by talking faster. "It was really more an emotional thing. Losing Madame and not knowing if—" She hesitated on the verge of saying something more.

Not knowing if you'd get away with her murder?

"But the first thing this morning, the nurse told me about Arnold Wynn committing suicide, and it may sound mean of me but I couldn't help feeling relieved. Because it really settles the whole thing about who could have killed Madame. Until then, I'd been so worried. What if one of the instructors was found guilty? That would have been the end of the spa."

You mean you were afraid Jason would have to take the rap? Lucy was tempted to say Arnold Wynn hadn't committed suicide, just to see Celia's reaction, but she didn't dare fly in the face of the inspector's warning. Better for us if Celia feels so safe now she isn't as careful.

203

But as Celia was turning to go, an irrepressible contrariness made Lucy say, "Did you know they're playing *Macbeth* again at the Connecticut Stratford next week? Marvelous cast. You and Jason ought to see it."

Celia's nostrils pinched in. "I don't know Mr. Pappas's plans, but I'll be much too busy with the memorial service for Madame."

A woman was hurrying down the back corridor just as Lucy came out of her room to go to the elevator. There was something so buoyant about the woman's walk—almost a stride—that for a second Lucy could hardly believe it was Adele.

"I was just coming to tell you the good news." Adele's voice was as buoyant as the rest of her. "Simms got our plane reservations for Zurich this morning, and I'm taking Lewis over on Tuesday."

Lucy said "How marvelous" before the catch in the plan struck her. She didn't like to ask straight out, "Have you cleared it with the inspector?" But she had to.

Adele seemed amused by the question. "Darling, I count on you to do that. You're the one he'll listen to. And what an attractive man he is, in an austere way. I was telling Lewis about him last night."

"I could tell Mac it's an emergency." Lucy was talking more to herself. "I'll say you don't dare put it off."

"Tell him whatever you think will do the trick. But we're going on Tuesday no matter. As soon as I heard about old Wynn killing himself, I knew that solved everything."

"But he—" Lucy caught herself and made a show of looking at her watch. "I'm due for a facial at eleven-thirty. I'll have to run."

Adele walked back down the corridor with her, still chattering. "She's fabulous, that operator. I ought to get in a session with her before we take off. But there's so much to do beforehand. Celia—bless her—has already arranged for their public-relations woman in Beverly Hills to take over for me here for a few weeks. And she's called the designer about doing the new exercise costumes. Did she see you this morning? She wanted to tell you herself."

"You'd already mentioned it to me yesterday noon."

"Oh, did I? My mind's a sieve. But now you can name your own fee. Why not stay here while I'm gone and finish the sketches?" She seemed to take Lucy's acceptance so for granted that she went right on. "I'll get on to the brochure the minute we're back from Zurich. I may even work on it there. And maybe Lewis will be well enough to do the layouts himself. Wouldn't that be exciting? Just like the old days."

Lucy nodded and tried to smile, but she felt suddenly heavy as lead, unable to soar into the dreamworld Adele was building. "I hear the elevator now. I'd better grab it."

Downstairs, the corridor was as bustling as it had been the morning before. One of the instructors—not Miss Tringle, a younger one; Lucy thought Miss Baskie—was presiding over the scales while another leggy interchangeable snaked the metal tape measure around thighs and midriffs. "A half-inch more gone! . . . And three whole pounds in twenty-four hours . . . But those upper thighs need work."

When the woman whose upper thighs needed work turned around, Lucy, like Terrizi, almost didn't recognize hay-hair in her sleek metamorphosis. "Oh, Mrs. Ramsdale, we're so glad it's all settled. I might have guessed the killer was an ex-husband. They can be so vindictive."

Marta Galt, who was sitting on a bench near the scales, said, "Vindictive's the word." Her wide mouth turned up at the corners as she glanced at Lucy. "Congratulations. And do give my best to Sergeant Terrizi." As Lucy came up to the bench, Marta murmured, "How much longer? Can't you wind it up today? Tell your inspector to push up his time schedule."

"You tell him. And while you're at it, tell him who to arrest."

"He already knows. Sergeant Terrizi said so."

Lucy stiffened. Terrizi hadn't told *her* any such thing. And that meant the inspector wanted her shut out. After all the cases she'd helped him solve, it was outrageous, arrogant, and stinking selfish.

"Just give me a hint who you've settled on. Is it—?" Marta mouthed the initials "C.G." so elaborately most of her teeth showed.

"You won't get a thing out of us till it's all over." Having covered up her own left-outedness, Lucy felt a human urge to show off. "What you were just doing—baring your teeth—is the best exercise I ever tried to keep from sagging." She bared her own teeth as if to snarl. Marta bared hers again, in imitation, and they faced each other, looking fierce.

"Girls!" Miss Baskie had turned, tape measure in hand. "You must *not* get worked up and lose your tempers. Remember the up-look of happiness."

"I was just showing Mrs. Galt a marvelous exercise to firm the jawline," Lucy said, moving closer and demonstrating again. She would have enjoyed actually biting Miss Baskie, but thought it might smack of bad taste. "It's good for your neck, too."

Crêpey-throat padded right over to watch, followed by hay-hair, and they, too, bared their teeth ferociously.

Marta said, "By God, it actually works. I can feel the muscles tighten."

Crêpey-throat said she wished she'd known about it twenty years ago. She bared her teeth even more savagely, as if to make up for lost time. Hay-hair, who was too busy making snarly faces to talk, bobbed her head in agreement.

"And here's another one I recommend." Lucy stuck out her tongue as far as it would go. The other three women instantly stuck out their tongues, too, eyes bulging. "Do it fifty times a day." As Lucy watched the flailing tongues, she felt gay and recharged, ready to tackle the operator who gave facials and to worm out secrets that would crack the case wide open.

The operator who gave facials wasn't that easy to worm. She was a large, muscular woman who wore clumping white shoes and a starched white uniform. Her pink-and-white face was still unlined, and her skin was remarkably good, but her blond hair looked as if it had been chopped around a bowl placed upside down on her head. She had the manner of a nanny who won't stand any nonsense but is willing to humor her charge, up to a point.

"If you'll take off that pretty dress, so we won't muck it up, and just slip into this robe that's big enough for three of you. Such a little lady to do those gorgeous drawings I heard about. Now we'll make you comfy on the recliner."

The recliner looked like a doctor's examining table with a backrest. Lucy was looking around for a footstool when the woman grabbed her under both arms and lifted her onto the thing as if she were three years old. "Just relax, dear. Is that back too high? Yes, we'll lower it a teensy to snuggle under your head. And we'll cover that silky hair of yours—natural curly, I can tell by the feel."

She was winding a headband deftly. "And when I roll this contraption up close, don't be scared and think it's a weapon from outer space." Actually, the machine looked more like something from the Hayden Planetarium. "It's just a Pore-o-scope magnifier, and you certainly don't have much to worry about. With skin like that, a baby should be so blessed."

As the woman peered, she made small sounds indicating first approval, then a series of clucks that were vaguely worrying. "Well, we *do* need some work there around the eyes."

Finally she rolled back the machine, which looked like a mounted telescope, and lathered cream on Lucy's face and throat. Her strong fingers moved in a rotating pattern, working it in, then light whiffling strokes around the eyes. "Now you lie back and think pretty thoughts while I mix up our special heated honey mask—Madame's own formula."

The word "mask" with "Madame" reminded Lucy forcibly of what she'd come for. She had just opened her mouth to say, Miss Simms tells me you were a great favorite of Madame's, when the operator turned, towel in hand, and wiped the cream off Lucy's face with astonishing speed. "Here we go. Shut your mouth. And your eyes."

The goo felt so hot on Lucy's face she had a hideous picture of herself in the After as Scarface. But almost at once the feeling changed to a delicious warmth that seemed to pervade her whole body. A blanket that felt like cashmere was tucked around her, and then the silence was deep and absolute. Lucy struggled to stay awake, but she could feel herself drifting off until the operator said in a faraway voice, "In the old days, I used to travel around the country with Madame, giving demonstrations in stores. And in the evenings she'd come to my room with some new batch of cream or a new liquid mask she'd want to try out. We'd put the stuff on each other and laugh like a couple of schoolgirls. I'd call her Velanie and she'd call me Helga-Svelga. But of course when we demonstrated before customers—"

Lucy was suddenly wide awake. "So she didn't mind letting strangers see her in a beauty mask?"

"Not strangers." The woman sounded shocked. "In the stores she might demonstrate a lipstick or eye shadow, and sometimes the creams, but never a mask. She'd use me as the model. In those days, I was worth looking at. And my skin—well, it's still not bad, at my age."

Lucy said quickly, "It's lovely. But when you say Madame wouldn't let strangers see her in a beauty mask—you don't mean people here at the spa, I mean the ones who worked for her."

"Only the old-timers. She was sensitive that way. And the older she got, the tougher she was about it."

"But would she have minded me seeing her that way?"

"You'd never get near her. She never even let the publicity people come in then. They learned that first thing: never barge in on Madame."

"How about Celia Grant?"

"Oh, well, Celia was like family. And how she worshipped Madame."

"Was Celia very upset when she came down here yesterday afternoon for a facial?"

"Shaken, you might say. And I happen to know she'd just had a set-to with Madame's ex-husband."

"Arnold Wynn?"

"Keep your eyes closed, dear. I shouldn't be talking to you like this but it's been on my mind. And when I heard that Arnold Wynn killed himself, I thought right away, He did it because he knew Celia was on to him."

"Did she tell you she thought Wynn was the murderer?"

"No. But just before her appointment I was having a

quick smoke on the balcony over the back entrance and I saw Celia coming in that way. I knew she didn't want any clients to see her in the corridor down here—it might have looked funny to them, the same day Madame was killed. Not that it isn't important to look your best no matter what comes, and after all, she had to set an example. Don't move your mouth, dear. Give the mask time to work. As I was saying, Celia was on her way in and that old sot Wynn came around the corner of the house and grabbed her. Scared her plenty. But Celia was giving as good as she got. They were standing there yelling at each other— Well, not yelling, but they looked like they wanted to. They were mad enough to spit."

"What were they saying?"

"Wynn kept talking about 'a bother' and how he'd told Madame."

Told Madame about Celia's mythical brother?

"He should talk about bother. He was always pestering Madame about money. I won't say he didn't have some reason. But to kill her—he must have been drunk as a loon."

"Do you think Celia accused him right out?"

"Well, the way he slunk off, my guess is she might have. I heard her say, 'Don't ever come near me again.' And she was trembling when she came in here, but she's not one to pour out her troubles. I didn't ask any questions, because she needed to unwind."

Lucy's head was spinning. How could Celia have poisoned Wynn's whiskey in the flask if she only saw him for those few minutes outside the door?

Who else had? Hilda Simms's voice came echoing back. ". . . shows how kind and thoughtful Mrs. Vining is."

A timer squawked, and Lucy jerked as if she'd been hit.

13

HILDA SIMMS had the *New York Times* on her desk, and as soon as the inspector came in she flourished it like a banner. "Did you see this picture of Madame? It wasn't her favorite photograph, but under the circumstances I think the *Times* did a wonderful job of assembling the story. They gave her a whole column and a half."

McDougal said he thought it was a very impressive obituary. And for Simms's sake he added, "I'm sure she deserved it."

The secretary was wearing a dark dress with a fresh white, too large collar, and above it her face had the caved-in look of somebody twenty years older.

McDougal felt considerably older himself, after a session that morning at the nursing home with Lewis Vining's doctor.

The doctor had said, "It's a thousand-to-one chance that the treatment will save Vining, but it's the only hope he has left. And I've urged it as much for the wife's sake as for Vining's. This way, even if he dies over there, she'll at least feel she's done everything possible. When I saw her night before last, she seemed to me on the verge of a breakdown. She's the sort who wants to wrestle the Fates with her own bare hands, and this will give her a sense that she's winning. For how long, I'd hate to guess."

McDougal, on his way out of the place afterward, had thought the grounds looked like a cemetery done in the carefully casual modern manner. He knew he was superimposing his own gloominess onto the scene; the prospect of having to tell Lucy the facts depressed him enormously.

He'd got back to the spa at twelve and been relieved to find the moment of unpleasant truth postponed. Sergeant Terrizi said Mrs. Ramsdale had told him she had an appointment for a facial at eleven-thirty downstairs and would see him about an hour later. Along with relief, the inspector had felt a certain masculine superiority because she was doing something so asininely frivolous.

On the way to see Hilda Simms, he'd knocked on Adele Vining's office door, not sure what he'd say if she answered, but having to know if she was or wasn't in. She wasn't.

Hilda Simms was folding the *Times* carefully, so as not to crease Madame's face. "There was something I wanted to ask you— Oh, I know. We want to have the memorial service Monday before Mrs. Vining leaves for Zurich, and the body should be cremated first, so I thought I'd better check with you."

"She'd planned to take her husband over that soon?" McDougal tried not to let the surprise show in his voice.

"Oh, it's all set. I got the reservations for Tuesday morning." Hilda Simms sounded more animated now. "So that's one happy piece of news I was able to give Mrs. Vining. She's been so anxious about her husband, and then Madame's death coming on top of it. I wasn't really sure Arnold Wynn's suicide solved everything until Mrs. Vining came to see me after she got back from the nursing home last night. She'd just heard about Arnold, and she said she should have suspected from the way he talked to her that he was guilty. He told her he'd been drinking that morning after he had a fight with Madame, and he didn't remember anything very clearly after that."

"What time did Mrs. Vining see him?"

"He went into her office right after he left me, around three-thirty. And Mrs. Vining was so sweet and comforting it made me feel ashamed I'd been so impatient with him. But now that I know he was guilty all along, I wish I'd kicked him in the teeth."

The picture of Hilda Simms doing a high kick aimed at the teeth gave McDougal a momentary flash of black humor. "Could you hear any part of their conversation?"

"Well, after I finished my Tokyo call, I couldn't help hearing a little. The wall is so thin between our two offices. Of course, Madame had hers soundproofed, but she thought that was terribly expensive so she didn't do Mrs. Vining's or mine. She was careful about money, you know. She—"

McDougal stopped her abruptly. "What exactly did you hear?"

His tone made the secretary flush. "I didn't put my ear to the wall to eavesdrop."

"Please, it's crucially important. If Arnold Wynn was telling her how guilty he felt, and confessing even in a roundabout way, you can see how that would tie up all loose ends so the authorities would be satisfied. You know how fussy the law can be about niggling details."

Hilda Simms's face opened up. "Oh, indeed I do. Those lawyers of Madame's—even about an unimportant contract."

"Can you tell me what Wynn said?"

"He was mumbly. But I'm sure Mrs. Vining would remember. She repeated part of it to me last night."

"I'll ask her. But I'd like to hear your version."

"Actually, I just heard what she was saying—bits of it. Of course, she didn't realize till later that he'd killed Madame or she wouldn't have been so kind."

"In what way was she kind?"

"I think she was trying to put herself on his level. For instance, she talked about how she was dying for a drink. She must have known it would be the cheapest kind of whiskey. He couldn't afford anything else, the amount he drank. I'm sure she just put the flask to her lips and pretended to drink."

And she'd be careful not to leave fingerprints, Mc-Dougal thought. Probably said, "Oh, I spilled some. I'm so awkward today"—and dried it off with a brisk rubbing. And dropped the poison in then. The picture was developing so sharply he almost missed what Simms was saying.

"It's odd your asking about this. Mrs. Ramdale was in here asking me the same things not fifteen minutes ago."

Fifteen minutes ago. But Lucy had said the facial took an hour, and it was just after twelve-thirty now. Something she'd mentioned the night before bobbed elusively in the back of McDougal's mind. Something about the operator who gave facials getting a bigger bequest in Velanie's will than Arnold Wynn.

"Tell me, this operator had known Velanie a long time?"

"Goodness, yes. Helga goes back further than any of us except poor Arnold. She and Madame used to go all around the country giving demonstrations in stores."

He thought he knew now why Lucy had gone for a

214

facial: Helga would know about the beauty mask, and about Velanie's longtime habits.

If Adele Vining had been next door while Lucy was asking Simms questions, if she'd heard even a few key words—"flask"—"mask."

"Do you remember if Mrs. Vining was in her office while Lucy was here with you?"

The secretary's long nose twitched as she thought. "Yes, she must have been. Because I think I remember her going out right after Mrs. Ramsdale left me. Yes, she did. I heard her running down the hall to catch up before Mrs. Ramsdale got to your office."

"My office?" he said numbly.

"Mrs. Ramsdale must have just missed you. She said she was on her way to see you."

And Adele must have overheard that, too. She'd had to stop Lucy in a hurry. Stop her how? She couldn't have knocked Lucy over the head in the corridor. And Lucy wouldn't have gone with her willingly. Not if she'd figured things out, as she must have.

The inspector jumped up so fast he knocked over the straight-backed chair he'd been sitting on. "Does Mrs. Vining have a gun?"

"Yes, indeed. She got a license to carry one because of having to drive back late at night from the nursing home. Did you want to borrow it?"

"For keeps." McDougal was already at the door. "This is desperately urgent. Call Sergeant Terrizi in my office. Tell him I think Mrs. Vining has Lucy. Ask him to meet me behind Vining's cottage. I'll be there as soon as I check Lucy's room . . . just in case." The last three words were a wishful mutter, more to himself.

"She killed Madame." It wasn't so much a question as a

215

stunned acceptance. When McDougal nodded, Simms, like an old war-horse, breathed fire. "We'll get her." As she reached for the house phone, she said, "What else can I do to help?"

"Pray."

The little pistol felt like a cannon pressed into Lucy's back.

"This time we'll go down the stairs," Adele said. "Everybody's gone to lunch by now, so we won't be interrupted."

"Adele, you're being ridiculously melodramatic." Lucy was doing her best to sound merely exasperated. "Why can't we have lunch while we talk? Let's go to my room and have the kitchen send over sandwiches." It was hard to chatter with the pistol digging into her back.

"Hurry." Adele nudged her to go down the stairs faster.

"I can't leap down two steps at a time. And stop poking me with that damn thing. It might go off, and then you'll be sorry."

"It won't go off unless I want it to."

The "unless" gave Lucy a spurt of hope. "Why don't you go wave it at Celia Grant? She's the one who killed Velanie and Wynn."

"Good try. It's unlucky for you I heard you asking Simms about the flask."

"Because I'd just learned from the woman who gives facials that Celia had taken a drink from it yesterday afternoon, so she could have dropped the poison in then."

"Celia doesn't drink. Save your breath and keep moving."

"Maybe Celia doesn't usually drink, but she took a drink out of Wynn's flask right outside the back entrance. And then they began yelling at each other and—"

"Celia never yells."

"Anybody can yell if they get mad enough."

"No, they can't. I had to take Velanie's abuse day after day without yelling back, and I took it for Lewis's sake."

"That must have been awful for you." For a second, Lucy felt a stab of real sympathy. They had reached the bottom of the stairs and she thought, How will Mac ever find me down here? Why didn't I wear beads so I could break the string and dribble them along like the heroine in that old Agatha Christie mystery?

As they started down the corridor, she thought wishfully of slipping off a shoe and leaving it as a clue. One trouble with that was she was wearing sneakers that tied on snugly. And, even if she'd been able to slide out of a pump, Adele would have noticed her limping along like a one-legged stork.

She saw the weighing machine ahead and thought longingly of how populated the corridor had been that morning. Then she had an idea. . . .

As they reached the scales, she stumbled, staggered against the wall, and righted herself by grabbing on to the weights bar.

The clang of the joggled steel weights made Adele furious. "You did that on purpose. Nobody's going to hear you." She was poking harder with the pistol, hustling Lucy on down the corridor.

"I couldn't help it. Honestly, Adele." Lucy made herself sound humble, which for her was quite a trick. "But I never had a pistol stuck in my back before. Haven't we gone far enough?"

"Keep going. You'll recognize it when we get there."

At the last door on the corridor, Adele said, "In here."

The first thing Lucy saw inside was the Pore-o-scope machine, and she had to fight an hysterical impulse to giggle. "Be sure to have Helga give you the hot honey mask before you go to Zurich."

The pistol wavered. "If I thought you'd let us take the plane and keep your mouth shut, I wouldn't have to kill you."

Lucy said too quickly, "I promise."

"You're lying. I can tell. Get up on that recliner."

"It's too high. I need a hand."

"Did you think I'd fall for that? And let you get the gun away? Crawl up any old way, but do it fast."

Lucy hauled herself up, making the process last as long as possible. The back of the recliner was still adjusted to fit her head—*Snuggle down and be cozy*—and she forced herself to lie back in a ludicrous semblance of lolling.

"Adele, why don't you at least sit down while we talk?"

"We won't be talking long."

"But even if you kill me, the inspector already knows you're the one."

"You're lying again. He thinks Wynn was a suicide. He said so."

"If Wynn was going to kill himself, he wouldn't have put the poison in his flask. McDougal just gave that out as a red herring. So help me God, that's the truth."

"Then I'll pin it on Jason. Yes, that's better anyway. Because then he'll be blamed for your death, too. I'd thought of making yours look like suicide but you're not the type. You're too conceited."

"Look who's talking," Lucy said, with heat. "You have the gall to think you can get away with three murders."

"You think I like killing you?" Adele's voice shrilled up. She's already over the edge, Lucy thought. Don't goad her. Stretch it out as long as you can. Dear God, bring McDougal down here fast.

"Velanie deserved it, and Wynn was no good to anyone. But I never wanted to kill you. Oh, Lucy, why did you have to meddle? We'd have worked together so well."

"You were the one who got the idea of hiring me in the first place. Velanie should have been grateful. On her phone call you taped—the one you played back to me after she was dead—Velanie was sounding so pleased."

Adele said sharply, "How did you learn about the tape?"

"It took me until today to figure it out." And I was lying right here on this damn recliner when Helga's timer went off and I finally caught on to how you'd worked your alibi. Aloud, she said, "If Velanie was so delighted, then what went wrong? Why did you have to kill her?"

The pistol in Adele's hand shook. "She was horrible. When I got in there, she said she wanted me to get on the booklet right away and get it out fast. I told her why I couldn't—that I had to take Lewis to Zurich first. His doctor had called and said it had to be now. Velanie said, 'Lewis is practically dead already. He's no good to you anyway.' And then she went on about how spending money for the Zurich treatments would just be a waste of her ten thousand. She said she might tell the bank I stole the money and have them block my account."

"That's monstrous." Just let me go on feeding you lines. The longer you talk the better.

The back of the recliner dug into her neck, and she thought, How did I ever relax on this thing before? "What did you tell her?"

"I had to say I'd get on the booklet first thing, and I went back to my office to work, but all I could think about was Lewis—how she'd wrecked his one chance to be cured. And finally I couldn't stand it any longer, so I went back to see her again. I thought I could make her under-

219

stand. But when I got in there she was snoozing upside down on that Yoga board. She looked inhuman—she *was* inhuman—and I knew she'd never give in. I hated her so much I just snatched up the dumbbell. Then afterward I felt awful when I saw the blood had splashed onto your sketch."

"You were sweet to clean it up." Kill somebody and then worry about spots on a sketch. You *are* crazy. Mac, Mac, where are you?

Adele's cottage was empty, and McDougal cursed himself for having taken the time to check it. "She'd have had to bring Lucy here at gunpoint," he said to Terrizi, "and she'd know somebody might see them on the way. And she'd have to get rid of the body in a hurry afterward so it wouldn't tie up with her. There's got to be someplace less risky for her. Christ! Am I stupid! Come on."

He was running back toward the main house, with Terrizi's short legs churning to keep up.

At the back entrance, McDougal said, "Remember what Celia Grant told us, about all the instructors going to lunch at the same time?" To the sergeant's bewilderment, the inspector was taking off his shoes. He motioned impatiently for Terrizi to do the same. "Can't make any sound from now on."

They crept down the stairs to the basement and stopped by the elevator to listen. Not a sound. When they started padding silently down the corridor, the inspector was in the lead, and as he went past the weighing machine, he stopped so abruptly the sergeant almost fell into him. McDougal didn't notice; he was pointing to the small gold wristwatch dangling on the end of the weights bar.

Lucy made herself look away from the gun toward the jars of cream on a shelf just to the left of Adele. It seemed fantastic that only a few hours before she'd been worried because the Pore-o-scope said she had lines under her eyes. *Oh, God, if I get out of here alive I'll never fuss about wrinkles again. And I'll never investigate a murder unless you specifically ask me to.* This last seemed unlikely, except perhaps in the next world.

When Lucy looked back at Adele, the gun seemed more on target than before. And Adele was sounding more and more strained.

"I'd promised Lewis that if the doctors told me it was hopeless I'd give him the poison. I kept it in my purse."

"You're so brave," Lucy said softly. "I couldn't have done that for Hal. I wouldn't even know how to get hold of the stuff in the first place."

Adele stiffened. "You're leading me on. You think if I talk enough your gangling inspector will find you before anything happens. I have to do it now. But I'm sorry, Lucy. Really I am."

"I know, it hurts you more than it does me." *Oh, Mac, I can't stall her any longer. This is our last chance.*

"Please, shut your eyes first."

"Haven't you got a blindfold for me?"

The gun jerked. "You could at least look away."

"Shall I look at the Pore-o-scope? That's a dying sight most people never get. Remind the newspapers to pick it up, as a fresh bit of color. Maybe you can arrange to make it look as if the Pore-o-scope fired the fatal shot."

"Jason's a safer bet. I told you, look away. It makes me nervous to have you staring right at me."

Lucy's eyes opened even wider. "How will Lewis like being married to a murderess?"

"He won't know. Nobody will. Lucy, for the last time, shut your eyes. Or look someplace else."

It was lucky that Lucy didn't. Otherwise she wouldn't have seen the door behind Adele inching open.

McDougal shouted to Lucy, "Duck!" as he grabbed Adele's arms from behind and forced her gun up.

The bullet smashed through the ceiling. And Adele screamed.

And went on screaming.

14

"How COULD I DUCK?" Lucy said. "If I'd rolled off that thing onto the floor, I might have fallen on my face and broken my nose. You wouldn't like me with a cauliflower nose."

"It's cauliflower ear," McDougal said. He was sitting at Lucy's kitchen table, using small pliers to take two links out of her watchband. "And I'd rather you had a squashed nose than a bullet through your head."

"Don't be so dogmatic. I didn't get either one." She was standing at the kitchen counter arranging sprays of monkshood, alias deadly nightshade, in a tall crystal vase. The flowers were the same violet blue as her eyes, and McDougal thought she looked like herself again, after two days at home.

"Which part of these things are poison—the flowers or the stems?"

"Both."

"I could mash them into a powder and take it to Adele to sprinkle on her cereal or something. If she hadn't used the poison capsule on Arnold Wynn, she could have saved it for herself after Lewis died on his own. You know what I think? She willed him to die that same night, so he wouldn't have to be told."

"He didn't have a chance anyway." The inspector thought it was a moment for stretching the truth a few notches. "His doctor told me he'd suggested the Zurich trip more for Adele's sake, because he thought she was about to crack up."

"She'd already cracked," Lucy said. "How could she believe we thought Arnold Wynn was a suicide when she'd put the poison in his *flask?*"

"When they get to that stage, they feel everybody else is stupid. And as far as Wynn was concerned, she was right. He was stupid and greedy, thinking he could blackmail a murderer. But he felt Velanie had gypped him, first by grabbing all his stock in the company, then in her will. So he wasn't interested in putting Adele in prison. He wanted her around to put the squeeze on whenever he was broke."

Lucy was staring out the window over the kitchen sink: two cardinals and three blue jays were squawking over which had first rights at the bird feeder. Normally she'd have rushed out to intercede on behalf of the cardinals, but right now she didn't even see them. She said, "I should have known what Wynn was after from the way he made me go through the whole bit about Velanie's phoning me and Adele taking me in there right afterward. He must have heard the recording five minutes before that— around twelve-thirty—Velanie's voice in Adele's office. And he knew how Velanie was about seeing outsiders when she had clay on her face. If only he'd kept his promise not to take another drink until after he saw you."

"That's like wishing he'd been a different kind of man to start with." McDougal nipped out the second link and reached for a cigarette. "At first, he meant to keep his word. He even told Adele he wouldn't take a drink himself till after he'd seen the inspector. That's when she knew it was safe to put the poison in his flask without having him drop dead right there in her office. She suggested the woods behind the tennis court as their meeting place because it was out of the way, and she knew he couldn't wait for her indefinitely without stoking his courage with whiskey. She'd promised to bring him a first big payment in cash; then she shifted her news conference to Wingate so she'd be well away from here, at the Oaks or the nursing home, when Wynn was found. She talked to me quite frankly about that, and about planning to make Jason the scapegoat if she needed one. She'd intended to plant the roll of Pliofilm in Velanie's cottage right after she brought back your sketch. But she heard somebody coming through from the main hall, so she dumped the roll inside the nearest door. I didn't ask her many more questions, because I was only allowed to see her for twenty minutes. They're keeping her sedated most of the time and she's still in the psychiatric wing. Her lawyer will probably plead insanity."

"Just so they don't let her loose for another twenty or thirty years." Lucy added another spray of monkshood to her bouquet, stepped back a few feet to gauge the effect, and nodded with satisfaction. "Even if she'd planted the Pliofilm on Jason, I wouldn't have thought he was guilty. I'd have thought it was Celia doing the 'Hell hath no fury' act. But I must say Adele was always good at improvising in a hurry."

"And she was the one who'd care about your sketch and try to salvage it. I couldn't imagine either Jason or Wynn taking that kind of pains. And to protect it with a Pliofilm cover—that suggested somebody who's been around artists and layouts—not Celia. Once I'd begun to suspect Adele, I went back over the interview in her office, and I remembered the tape recorder on her desk. That would explain why you were so positive you were hearing Velanie on the phone: it was Velanie. And you spotted the muzziness in her voice, so you experimented that night with the beauty clay."

Lucy nodded dejectedly. "And got the wrong answer. It wasn't until I was lying on that damn recliner with clay on my face, and Helga said Velanie never even saw her publicity people when she was gopped up. Then the timer buzzed and the whole thing clicked in my head. I remembered that Adele picked up Velanie's timer right after we found the body. I think she'd forgotten to wipe off her fingerprints after she reset it, so she wanted a reason for handling it again. I was an idiot not to spot the trick right away. And I knew Adele had a tape recorder she used all the time. And I knew at first it was Velanie's voice on the phone, but she had to be dead by then, so somebody else was imitating her. I'm getting too old to play detective."

It was the first time she'd used a phrase like "play detective," and McDougal knew that for Lucy to belittle herself was an ominous sign.

He said firmly, "That's nonsense. You're a natural." He snapped the clasp shut on the shortened watchband. "If you hadn't had the wits to hang this on the scales—" He got up and handed it to her with what might have been construed as a slight bow. "For courage and quick thinking above and beyond the call of duty."

Coming from Inspector James McDougal, it was an extraordinarily fulsome performance.

Lucy seemed to take it in stride. She said kindly, "Well,

you were the one who spoiled her aim. That bullet—"
She began to laugh rather wildly, and McDougal wondered if he'd have to slap her. She hadn't been hysterical up to now, not even when the gun had gone off.

"I forgot to tell you before." Lucy had to stop to dry her streaming eyes with a paper towel. "Marta Galt told me. They'd all come from lunch that day and several of them were standing in the back hall talking. One of the women said that whenever there was trouble at home, her analyst always advised her to get away and spend a week or two in a reducing spa where she could unwind and forget everything else. She was saying she could hardly wait to tell him about Velanie being murdered when bang, the bullet from Adele's gun shot through the floor, right past her. The woman reared back and said, 'Wait till I tell my analyst *this*.' "

McDougal laughed obligingly.

"Marta's coming up for the wedding."

Wedding! The inspector, understandably, got his wind up. How had Marta Galt got the notion that he and his landlady were—

"If Angie's mother finally lets it happen. Terrizi told Marta September."

McDougal should have been relieved, but somehow he felt let down.

"And Marta wants us to be on her show to talk about the murders."

"That's out of the question. I wouldn't consider it."

He braced himself for one of Lucy's temper tantrums, but she only shrugged. "O.K. I'll ask Nicky to appear with me. He'd be very good."

She picked up a long-handled fork, turned to the stove, and lifted the lid of a cast-iron Dutch oven. As she poked into its contents, the aroma of beef and brandy and herbs drifted past his nostrils.

After a long silence, he said, "I might if they didn't try to put makeup on me."

"You wouldn't even need a hairpiece. That's unusual for a man your age. Now, if you'll open the wine."